DOVER MYSTERY CLASSICS

THE CASE OF JENNIE BRICE

MARY ROBERTS RINEHART

DOVER PUBLICATIONS, INC.
Mineola, New York

Bibliographical Note

This Dover edition, first published in 2017, is an unabridged republication of the work originally published by Rinehart and Company, Inc., New York, in 1913.

International Standard Book Number

ISBN-13: 978-0-486-81946-4
ISBN-10: 0-486-81946-9

Manufactured in the United States by LSC Communications
81946902   2020
www.doverpublications.com

CHAPTER 1

We have just had another flood, bad enough, but only a foot or two of water on the first floor. Yesterday we got the mud shoveled out of the cellar and found Peter, the spaniel Mr. Ladley left when he "went away." The flood, and the fact that it was Mr. Ladley's dog whose body was found half buried in the basement fruit closet, brought back to me the strange events of the other flood five years ago, when the water reached more than halfway to the second story and brought with it to some, mystery and sudden death, and to me the worst case of "shingles" I have ever seen.

My name is Pitman in this narrative. It is not really Pitman, but that does well enough. I belong to an old Pittsburgh family. I was born on Penn Avenue, when that was the best part of town, and I lived until I was fifteen very close to what is now the Pittsburgh Club. It was a dwelling then. I have forgotten who lived there.

I was a girl in 'seventy-seven during the railroad riots, and I recall our driving in the family carriage over to one of the Allegheny hills, and seeing the yards burning and the sound of shooting from across the river. It was the next year that I ran away from school to marry Mr. Pitman, and I have not known my family since. We were never reconciled, although I came back to Pittsburgh after twenty years of wandering. Mr. Pitman was dead. The old city called me, and I came. I had a hundred dollars or so, and I took a house in lower Allegheny where, because they are partly inundated every spring rents are cheap, and I kept boarders. My house was always orderly and clean, and although the neighborhood had a bad name a good many theatrical people stopped with me. Five minutes across the bridge and they were in the theater district. Allegheny at that time was still an independent city. But since then it has allied itself with Pittsburgh. It is now the North Side.

I was glad to get back. I worked hard, but I made my rent and my living, and a little over. Now and then on summer evenings I went to one of the parks and sitting on a bench watched the children playing around, and looked at my sister's house, closed for the summer. It is a very large house; her butler once had his wife boarding with me—a nice little woman.

It is curious to recall that at that time five years ago I had never seen my niece, Lida Harvey, and then to think that only the day before yesterday she came in her car as far as she dared, and then sat there waving to me, while the police patrol brought across in a skiff a basket of provisions she had sent me.

I wonder what she would have thought had she known that the elderly woman in a calico wrapper with an old overcoat over it and wearing a pair of rubber boots was her full aunt!

The flood and the sight of Lida both brought back the case of Jennie Brice. For even then Lida and Mr. Howell were interested in each other.

This is April. The flood I am writing about five years ago was earlier, in March. It had been a long hard winter, with ice gorges in all the upper valley. Then in early March there came a thaw. The gorges broke up and began to come down, filling the rivers with crushing grinding ice.

There are three rivers at Pittsburgh, the Allegheny and the Monongahela uniting there at the Point to form the Ohio. And all three were covered with broken ice, logs, and all sorts of debris from the upper valleys.

A warning was sent out from the weather bureau, and I got my carpets ready to lift that morning. That was on the fourth of March, a Sunday. Mr. Ladley and his wife, Jennie Brice, had the parlor bedroom and the room behind it. Mrs. Ladley, or Miss Brice as she preferred to be known, had a small part at a local theater which kept a permanent stock company. Her husband was in the same business, but he was not working that season. It was the wife who paid the bills, and a lot of quarreling they did about it.

I knocked at the door at ten o'clock, and Mr. Ladley opened it. He was a short man, rather stout and getting bald, and he always had a cigarette in his mouth. Even yet, the parlor smells of them in damp weather.

"What do you want?" he asked sharply, holding the door open about an inch.

"The water's coming up very fast, Mr. Ladley," I said. "It's up to the swinging shelf in the cellar now. I'd like to take up the carpet and move the piano."

"Come back in an hour or so," he snapped, and tried to close the door. But I had got my toe in the crack.

"I'll have to have the piano moved, Mr. Ladley," I said. "You'd better put off what you're doing."

I thought he was probably writing. He spent most of the day writing, using the washstand as a desk, and it kept me busy with oxalic acid taking ink spots out of the splasher and the towels. He was writing a play, and talked a lot about the Shuberts having promised to star him in it when it was finished.

"Hell!" he said, and turning spoke to somebody in the room.

"We can go into the back room," I heard him say, and he closed the door. When he opened it again the room was empty. I called in Terry, the Irishman who does odd jobs for me now and then, and we both got to work at the tacks in the carpet, Terry working by the window and I by the door into the back parlor, which the Ladleys used as a bedroom.

That was how I happened to hear what I afterward told the police.

Someone, a man but not Mr. Ladley, was talking. Mrs. Ladley broke in. "I won't do it!" she said flatly. "Why should I help him? He doesn't help me. He loafs here all day, smoking and sleeping, and sits up all night drinking and keeping me awake."

The voice went on again, as if in reply to this, and I heard a rattle of glasses as if they were pouring drinks. They always had whisky, even when they were behind with their board.

"That's all very well," Mrs. Ladley said. I could always hear her, since she had the theatrical sort of voice which carries. "But what about the prying she-devil that runs the house?"

"Hush, for God's sake!" broke in Mr. Ladley, and after that they spoke in whispers. Even with my ear against the panel I could not catch a word.

The men came just then to move the piano, and by the time we had taken it and the furniture upstairs the water was over the kitchen floor, and creeping forward into the hall. I had never seen the river come up so fast. By noon the yard was full of floating ice, and at three that afternoon the police skiff was on the front street, and I was wading around in rubber boots, taking the pictures off the walls.

I was too busy to see who the Ladleys' visitor was, and he had gone when I remembered him again. The Ladleys took the second-story front, which was empty, and Mr. Reynolds who was in the silk department in a store across the river had the room just behind.

I put up a coal stove in a back room next the bathroom, and managed to cook the dinner there. I was washing up the dishes when Mr. Reynolds came in. As it was Sunday he was in his slippers, and he had the colored supplement of a morning paper in his hand.

"What's the matter with the Ladleys?" he asked. "I can't read for their quarreling."

"Booze, probably," I said. "When you've lived in the flood district as long as I have, Mr. Reynolds, you'll know that the rising of the river is a signal for every man in the vicinity to stop work and get tight. The fuller the river, the fuller the male population."

"Then this flood will likely make 'em drink themselves to death!" he said. "It's a lulu."

"It's the neighborhood's annual debauch. The women are busy keeping the babies from getting drowned in the cellars, or they'd get full too. Since it's come this far I hope it will come farther, so the landlord will have to paper the parlor."

That was at three o'clock. At four Mr. Ladley went down the stairs, and I heard him getting into a skiff in the lower hall. There were boats going back and forth all the time, carrying crowds of curious people, and taking the flood sufferers to the corner grocery, where they were lowering groceries in a basket on a rope from an upper window.

I had been making tea when I heard Mr. Ladley go out. I fixed a tray with a cup of it and some crackers and took it to their door. I had never liked Mrs. Ladley, but it was chilly in the house with the gas shut off and the lower floor full of ice water. And it is hard enough to keep boarders in the flood district.

She did not answer to my knock, so I opened the door and went in. She was at the window, looking after him, and the brown valise which figured in the case later was open on the floor. Over the foot of the bed was the black and white dress with the red collar.

When I spoke to her she turned around quickly. She was a tall woman, about twenty-eight, with very white teeth and yellow hair, which she parted a little to one side and drew down over her ears. She had a sullen face and large well-shaped hands, with her nails long and very pointed.

"The she-devil has brought you some tea," I said. "Where shall she put it?"

"She-devil!" she repeated, raising her eyebrows. "It's a very thoughtful she-devil. Who called you that?"

But what with the sight of the valise and the fear that they might be leaving, I thought it best not to quarrel. She had left the window, and going to her dressing table had picked up her nail file.

"Never mind," I said. "I hope you are not going away. These floods don't last, and they're really a benefit. Plenty of the people around here rely on them every year to wash out their cellars."

"No, I'm not going away," she replied lazily. "I'm taking that dress to Miss Hope at the theater. She is going to wear it in *Charlie's Aunt* next week. She hasn't half enough of a wardrobe to play leads in stock. Look at this thumbnail, broken to the quick!"

If I had only looked to see which thumb it was! But I was putting the tea tray on the washstand and moving Mr. Ladley's papers to find room for it. Peter, the spaniel, begged for a lump of sugar and I gave it to him.

"Where is Mr. Ladley?" I asked.

"Gone out to see the river."

"I hope he'll be careful. There's a drowning or two every year in these floods."

"Then I hope he won't," she said calmly. "Do you know what I was doing when you came in? I was looking after his boat and hoping it had a hole in it."

"You won't feel that way tomorrow, Mrs. Ladley," I protested, shocked. "You're just nervous and worn out. Most men have their ugly times. Many a time I wished Mr. Pitman was gone—until he went. Then I'd have given a good bit to have him back again."

She was standing in front of the dresser fixing her hair. She turned and looked at me over her shoulder.

"Probably Mr. Pitman was a man," she said. "My husband is a fiend, a devil."

Well, a good many women have said that to me at different times. But just let me say such a thing to them, or repeat their own words to them the next day, and they would fly at me in a fury. So I said nothing, and put the cream into her tea.

I never saw her again.

CHAPTER 2

There is not much sleeping done in the flood district during a spring flood. The gas and electric lights were shut off, and I gave Mr. Reynolds and the Ladleys each a lamp. I sat in the back room I had made into a temporary kitchen, with a candle and with a bedquilt around my shoulders. The water rose fast in the lower hall, but by midnight at the seventh step it stopped rising and stood still. I always have a skiff during the flood season, and as the water rose I tied it to one spindle of the staircase after another.

I made myself a cup of tea, and at one o'clock I stretched out on a sofa for a few hours' sleep. I think I had been sleeping only an hour or so when someone touched me on the shoulder and I started up. It was Mr. Reynolds, partly dressed.

"Someone has been in the house, Mrs. Pitman," he said. "They went away just now in the boat."

"Perhaps it was Peter," I suggested drowsily. "That dog is always wandering around at night."

"Not unless Peter can row a boat," said Mr. Reynolds dryly.

I got up, being already fully dressed, and taking the candle we went to the staircase. I noticed it was a minute or so after two o'clock as we left the room. The boat was gone, not untied, but cut loose. The end of the rope was still fastened to the stair rail. I sat down on the stairs and looked at Mr. Reynolds.

"It's gone!" I said. "If the house catches fire we'll have to drown."

"It's rather curious, when you consider it." We both spoke softly, not to disturb the Ladleys. "I've been awake, and I heard no boat come in. Yet, if no one came in a boat, and came from the street, they would have had to swim in."

I felt queer and creepy. The street door was open, of course, and there was some light outside. It gave me a strange feeling to sit there in the darkness on the stairs, with the arch of the front door like the entrance to a cavern, and see now and then a chunk of ice slide into view, turn around in the eddy, and pass on. It was bitter cold too, and the wind was rising.

"I'll go through the house," said Mr. Reynolds. "There's likely nothing worse the matter than some drunken mill hand on a vacation while the mills are underwater. But I'd better look."

He left me, and I sat there alone in the darkness. I had a presentiment of something wrong, but I tried to think it was only discomfort and the cold. The water, driven in by the wind, swirled at my feet. And something dark floated in and lodged on the step below. I reached down and touched it. It was a dead kitten. I had never known a dead cat to bring me anything but bad luck, and here was one washed in at my very feet.

Mr. Reynolds came back soon, and reported the house quiet and in order.

"But I found Peter shut up in one of the third-floor rooms," he said, "and let him out. Did you put him there?"

I had not, and said so; but as the dog went everywhere, and the door might have blown shut, we did not attach much importance to that at the time.

Well, the skiff was gone, and there was no use worrying about it until morning. I went back to the sofa to keep warm, but I left my candle lighted and my door open. I did not sleep. The dead cat was on my mind, and as if it were not bad enough to have it washed in at my feet, about four in the morning Peter, prowling uneasily, discovered it and brought it in and put it on my couch, wet and stiff, poor little thing!

I looked at the clock. It was a quarter after four, and except for the occasional crunch of one ice cake hitting another in the yard everything was quiet. And then I heard the stealthy sound of oars in the lower hall.

I am not a brave woman. I lay there, hoping Mr. Reynolds would hear and open his door. But he was sleeping soundly. Peter snarled and ran out into the hall, and the next moment I heard Mr. Ladley speaking. "Down, Peter," he said. "Down. Go and lie down."

I took my candle and went out into the hall. Mr. Ladley was stooping over the boat, trying to tie it to the staircase. The rope was short, having been cut, and he was having trouble. Perhaps it was the candlelight, but he looked ghost-white and haggard.

"I borrowed your boat, Mrs. Pitman," he said, civilly enough. "Mrs. Ladley was not well, and I went to the drugstore."

"You've been more than two hours going to the drugstore," I said.

He muttered something about not finding any open at first, and went into his room. He closed and locked the door behind him, and although Peter whined and scratched he did not let him in.

He looked so agitated that I thought I had been harsh, and that perhaps she was really ill. I knocked at the door and asked if I could do anything. But he only called "No" curtly through the door, and asked me to take that infernal dog away.

I went back to the sofa and tried to sleep, for the water had dropped an inch or so on the stairs and I knew the danger was over. Peter came shivering at dawn and got on the sofa with me. I put an end of the quilt over him, and he stopped shivering after a time and went to sleep.

The dog was company. I lay there, wide awake, thinking about Mr. Pitman's death; and how I had come, by degrees, to be keeping a cheap boardinghouse in the flood district, and to having to take impudence from everybody who chose to rent a room from me, and to being called a she-devil. From that I got to thinking again about the Ladleys, and how she had said he was a fiend, and to doubting about his having gone out for medicine for her. I dozed off again at daylight, and being worn out I slept heavily.

At seven o'clock Mr. Reynolds came to the door, dressed for the store. He was a tall man of about fifty, neat and orderly in his habits, and he always remembered that I had seen better days, and treated me as a lady.

"Never mind about breakfast for me this morning, Mrs. Pitman," he said. "I'll get a cup of coffee at the other end of the bridge. I'll take the boat and send it back with Terry."

He turned and went along the hall and down to the boat. I heard him push off from the stairs with an oar and row out into the street. Peter followed him to the stairs.

At a quarter after seven Mr. Ladley came out and called to me: "Just bring in a cup of coffee and some toast," he said. "Enough for one."

He went back and slammed his door, and I made his coffee. I steeped a cup of tea for Mrs. Ladley at the same time. He opened the door just wide enough for the tray, and took it without so much as a "thank you." He had a cigarette in his mouth as usual, and I could see a fire in the grate and smell something like scorching cloth.

"I hope Mrs. Ladley is better," I said, getting my foot in the crack of the door so he could not quite close it. It smelled to me as if he had accidentally set fire to something with his cigarette, and I tried to see into the room.

"What about Mrs. Ladley?" he snapped.

"You said she was ill last night."

"Oh, yes! Well, she wasn't very sick. She's better."

"Shall I bring her some tea?"

"Take your foot away!" he ordered. "No. She doesn't want tea. She's not here."

"Not here!"

"Good heavens!" he snarled. "Is her going away anything to make such a fuss about? The Lord knows I'd be glad to get out of this infernal pig-wallow myself."

"If you mean my house—" I began.

But he had pulled himself together and was more polite when he answered. "I mean the neighborhood. Your house is all that could be desired for the money. If we don't have linen sheets and double cream, at least we're paying muslin and milk prices."

Either my nose was growing accustomed to the odor or it was dying away. I took my foot away from the door. "When did Mrs. Ladley leave?" I asked.

"This morning, very early. I rowed her to Federal Street."

"You couldn't have had much sleep," I said dryly. For he looked horrible. There were lines around his eyes, which were red, and his lips looked dry and cracked.

"She's not in the piece this week at the theater," he said, licking his lips and looking past me, not at me. "She'll be back by Saturday."

I did not believe him. I do not think he imagined I did. He shut the door in my face, and it caught poor Peter by the nose. The dog ran off howling, but although Mr. Ladley had been as fond of the animal as it was in his nature to be fond of anything he paid no attention. As I started down the hall after him, I saw what Peter had been carrying—a slipper of Mrs. Ladley's. It was soaked with water. Evidently Peter had found it floating at the foot of the stairs.

Although the idea of murder had not entered my head at that time, the slipper gave me a turn. I picked it up and looked at it, a black one with a beaded toe, short in the vamp and high heeled, the sort most actresses wear. Then I went back and knocked at the door of the front room again.

"What the devil do you want now?" he called from beyond the door.

"Here's a slipper of Mrs. Ladley's," I said. "Peter found it floating in the lower hall."

He opened the door wide and let me in. The room was in tolerable order, much better than when Mrs. Ladley was about. He looked at the slipper, but he did not touch it. "I don't think that's hers," he said.

"I've seen her wear it a hundred times."

"Well, she'll never wear it again." And then seeing me stare he added: "It's ruined with the water. Throw it out. And by the way I'm sorry, but I set fire to one of the pillow slips—dropped asleep, and my cigarette did the rest. Just put it on the bill."

He pointed to the bed. One of the pillows had no slip, and the ticking cover had a scorch or two on it. I went over and looked at it.

"The pillow will have to be paid for too, Mr. Ladley," I said. "And there's a sign nailed on the door that forbids smoking in bed. If you are going to set fire to things I shall have to charge extra."

"Really!" he jeered, looking at me with his cold fishy eyes. "Is there any sign on the door saying that boarders are charged extra for seven feet of filthy river in the bedrooms?"

I was never a match for him, and I make it a principle never to bandy words with my boarders. I took the pillow and the slipper and went out. The telephone was ringing on the stair landing. It was the theater, asking for Miss Brice.

"She has gone away," I said.

"What do you mean? Moved away?"

"Gone for a few days' vacation," I replied. "She isn't playing this week, is she?"

"Wait a moment," said the voice. There was a hum of conversation from the other end, and then another man came to the telephone.

"Can you find out where Miss Brice has gone?"

"I'll see."

I went to Ladley's door and knocked. Mr. Ladley opened it a crack and answered from just beyond.

"The theater is asking where Mrs. Ladley is."

"Tell them I don't know," he snarled, and shut the door. I took his message to the telephone.

Whoever it was swore and hung up the receiver.

All the morning I was uneasy, I hardly knew why. Peter felt it as I did. There was no sound from the Ladleys' room, and the house was quiet, except for the lapping water on the stairs and the police patrol going back and forth.

At eleven o'clock a boy in the neighborhood, paddling on a raft, fell into the water and was drowned. I watched the police boat go past carrying his little cold body, and after that I was good for nothing. I went and sat with Peter on the stairs. The dog's conduct had been strange all morning. He had sat just above the water, looking at it and whimpering. Perhaps he was expecting another kitten, or—

It is hard to say how ideas first enter one's mind. But the notion that Mr. Ladley had killed his wife and thrown her body into the water came to me as I sat there. All at once I seemed to see it all:

the quarreling the day before, the night trip in the boat, the water-soaked slipper, his haggard face that morning, even the way the spaniel sat and stared at the flood.

Terry brought the boat back at half past eleven, towing it behind another.

"Well," I said, from the stairs, "I hope you've had a pleasant morning."

"What doing?" he asked, not looking at me.

"Rowing about the streets. You've had that boat for hours."

He tied it up without a word to me, but he spoke to the dog. "Good morning, Peter," he said. "It's nice weather for fishes, ain't it?"

He picked out a bit of floating wood from the water, and showing it to the dog, flung it into the parlor. Peter went after it with a splash. He was pretty fat, and when he came back I heard him wheezing. But what he brought back was not the stick of wood. It was the knife I use for cutting bread. It had been on a shelf in the room where I had slept the night before, and now Peter brought it out of the flood where its wooden handle had kept it afloat. The blade was broken off short.

It is not unusual to find one's household goods floating around during floodtime. More than once I've lost a chair, and seen it after the water had gone down, new scrubbed and painted, in Molly Maguire's kitchen next door. And perhaps now and then a bit of luck would come to me, a dog kennel or a chicken house or a kitchen table, or even as happened once a month-old baby in a wooden cradle which lodged against my back fence and had come forty miles, as it turned out, with no worse mishap than a cold in its head.

But the knife was different. I had put it on the mantel over the stove I was using upstairs the night before, and I hadn't touched it since. As I sat staring at it, Terry took it from Peter and handed it to me.

"Better give me a penny, Mrs. Pitman," he said in his impudent Irish way. "I hate to give you a knife. It may cut our friendship."

I reached over to hit him a clout on the head, but I did not. The sunlight was coming in through the window at the top of the stairs and shining on the rope that was tied to the banister. The end of the rope was covered with stains, brown with a glint of red in them.

I got up shivering. "You can get the meat at the butcher's, Terry," I said, "and come back for me in a half hour." Then I turned and went upstairs, weak in the knees, to put on my hat and coat. I had made up my mind that there had been murder done.

CHAPTER 3

I looked at my clock as I went downstairs. It was just twelve-thirty. I thought of telephoning for Mr. Reynolds to meet me, but it was his lunch hour, and besides I was afraid to telephone from the house while Mr. Ladley was in it.

Peter had been whining again. When I came down the stairs he had stopped whimpering and was wagging his tail. A strange boat had put into the hallway and was coming back.

"Now, old boy!" somebody was saying from the boat. "Steady, old chap! I've got something for you."

A little man, elderly and alert, was standing up in the boat, poling it along with an oar. Peter gave vent to joyful yelps. The elderly gentleman brought his boat to a stop at the foot of the stairs, and reaching down into a tub at his feet held up a large piece of raw liver. Peter almost went crazy, and I remembered suddenly that I had forgotten to feed the poor beast for more than a day.

"Would you like it?" asked the gentleman. Peter sat up, as he had been taught to do, and barked. The gentleman reached down again, got a wooden platter from a stack of them at his feet, and placing the liver on it put it on the step. The whole thing was so neat and businesslike that I could only stare.

"That's a well-trained dog, madam," said the elderly gentleman, beaming at Peter over his glasses. "You should not have neglected him."

"The flood put him out of my mind," I explained, humbly enough, for I was ashamed.

"Exactly. Do you know how many starving dogs and cats I have found this morning?" He took a notebook out of his pocket and glanced at it. "Forty-eight dogs. Forty-eight, madam! And ninety-three cats! I have found them marooned in trees, clinging to fences, floating on barrels, and I have found them in comfortable houses where there was no excuse for their neglect. Well, I must be moving on. I have the report of a cat with a new litter in the loft of a stable near here."

He wiped his hands carefully on a fresh paper napkin, of which also a heap rested on one of the seats of the boat, and picked up an oar, smiling benevolently at Peter. Then suddenly he bent over and looked at the stained rope end, tied to the stair rail.

"What's that?" he said.

"That's what I'm going to find out," I replied. I glanced up at the Ladleys' door, but it was closed.

The little man dropped his oar, and fumbling in his pockets pulled out a small magnifying glass. He bent over, holding to the rail, and inspected the stains with the glass. I had taken a fancy to him at once, and in spite of my excitement I had to smile a little.

"Humph!" he said, and looked up at me. "That's blood. Why did you *cut* the boat loose?"

"I didn't," I said. "If that is blood, I want to know how it got there. That was a new rope last night." I glanced at the Ladleys' door again, and he followed my eyes.

"I wonder," he said, raising his voice a little, "if I come into your kitchen, if you will allow me to fry a little of that liver. There's a wretched Maltese in a tree at the corner of Fourth Street that won't touch it raw."

I saw that he wanted to talk to me, so I turned around and led the way to the temporary kitchen I had made.

"Now," he said briskly, when he had closed the door, "there's something wrong here. Perhaps if you tell me I can help. If I can't it will do you good to talk about it. My name's Holcombe, retired merchant. Apply to First National Bank for references."

"I'm not sure there *is* anything wrong," I began. "I guess I'm only nervous, and thinking little things are big ones. There's nothing to tell."

"Nonsense. I come down the street in my boat. A white-faced gentleman with a cigarette looks out from a window when I stop at the door, and ducks back when I glance up. I come in and find a pet dog, obviously overfed at ordinary times, whining with hunger on the stairs. As I prepare to feed him a pale woman comes down, trying to put a right-hand glove on her left hand, and with her jacket wrong side out. What am I to think?"

I started and looked at my coat. He was right. And when as I tried to take it off he helped me, and even patted me on the shoulder—what with his kindness, and the long morning alone worrying and the sleepless night—I began to cry. He had a clean handkerchief in my hand before I had time to think of one.

"That's it," he said. "It will do you good, only don't make a noise about it. If it's a husband on the annual flood spree, don't worry, madam. They always come around in time to whitewash the cellars."

"It isn't a husband," I sniffled.

"Tell me about it," he said. There was something so kindly in his face, and it was so long since I had had a bit of human sympathy, that I almost broke down again.

I sat there, with a crowd of children paddling on a raft outside the window, and Molly Maguire next door hauling the morning's milk up in a pail fastened to a rope, her doorway being too narrow to admit the milkman's boat, and I told him the whole story.

"Humph!" he exclaimed, when I had finished. "It's curious, but—you can't prove a murder unless you can produce a body."

"When the river goes down we'll find the body," I said, shivering. "It's in the parlor."

"Then why doesn't he try to get away?"

"He is ready to go now. He only went back when your boat came in."

Mr. Holcombe went to the door, and flinging it open peered into the lower hall. He was too late. His boat was gone, tub of liver, pile of wooden platters and all!

We hurried to the room the Ladleys had occupied. It was empty. From the window as we looked out we could see the boat, almost a square away. It had stopped where, the street being higher, a doorstep rose above the flood. On the step was sitting a forlorn yellow puppy. As we stared Mr. Ladley stopped the boat, looked back at us, bent over, placed a piece of liver on a platter and reached it over to the dog. Then rising in the boat he bowed, with his hat over his heart, in our direction, sat down calmly and rowed around the corner out of sight.

Mr. Holcombe was in a frenzy of rage. He jumped up and down, shaking his fist out the window after the retreating boat. He ran down the staircase, only to come back and look out the window again. The police boat was not in sight, but the Maguire children had worked their raft around to the street and were under the window. He leaned out and called to them.

"A quarter each, boys," he said, "if you'll take me on that raft to the nearest pavement."

"Money first," said the oldest boy, holding his cap.

But Mr. Holcombe did not wait. He swung out over the window sill, holding by his hands, and lit fairly in the center of the raft.

"Don't touch anything in that room until I come back," he called to me, and jerking the pole from one of the boys propelled the raft with amazing speed down the street.

The liver on the stove was burning. There was a smell of scorching through the rooms and a sort of bluish haze smoke. I hurried back and took it off. By the time I had cleaned the pan Mr. Holcombe was back again, in his own boat. He had found it at the end of the next street, where the flood ceased, but no sign of Ladley anywhere. He had not seen the police boat.

"Perhaps that is just as well," he said philosophically. "We can't go to the police with a wet slipper and a bloodstained rope and accuse a man of murder. We have to have a body."

"He killed her," I said obstinately. "She told me yesterday he was a fiend. He killed her and threw the body in the water."

"Very likely. But he didn't throw it here."

In spite of that, however, he went over all the lower hall with his boat, feeling every foot of the floor with an oar, and finally at the back end he looked up at me as I stood on the stairs.

"There's something here," he said.

I went cold all over and had to clutch the railing. But when Terry had come, and the two of them brought the thing to the surface, it was only the dining-room rug, which I had rolled up and forgotten to carry upstairs!

At half past one Mr. Holcombe wrote a note and sent it off with Terry, and borrowing my boots, which had been Mr. Pitman's, investigated the dining room and kitchen from a floating plank. The doors were too narrow to admit the boat. But he found nothing more important than a rolling pin. He was apparently not at all depressed by his failure. He came back drenched to the skin about three, and asked permission to search the Ladleys' bedroom.

"I have a friend coming pretty soon, Mrs. Pitman," he said, "a young newspaperman named Howell. He's a nice boy, and if there is anything to this I'd like him to have it for his paper. He and I have been having some arguments about circumstantial evidence too, and I know he'd like to work on this."

I gave him a pair of Mr. Pitman's socks, for his own were saturated, and while he was changing them the telephone rang. It was the theater again, asking for Jennie Brice.

"You are certain she is out of the city?" someone asked, the same voice as in the morning.

"Her husband says so."

"Ask him to come to the phone."

"He is not here."

"When do you expect him back?"

"I'm not sure he is coming back."

"Look here," said the voice angrily, "can't you give me any satisfaction? Or don't you care to?"

"I've told you all I know."

"You don't know where she is?"

"No, sir."

"She didn't say she was coming back to rehearse for next week's piece?"

"Her husband said she went away for a few days' rest. He left here about noon and hasn't come back. That's all I know, except that they owe me three weeks' rent I'd like to get hold of."

The owner of the voice hung up the receiver with a snap, and left me pondering. It seemed to me that Mr. Ladley had been very reckless. Did he expect anyone to believe that Jennie Brice had gone for a vacation without notifying the theater? Especially when she was to rehearse that week? I thought it curious, to say the least. I went back and told Mr. Holcombe, who put it down in his notebook, and together we went to the Ladleys' room.

The room was in better order than usual, as I have said. The bed was made—which was out of the ordinary, for Jennie Brice never made a bed—but made the way a man makes one, with the blankets wrinkled and crooked beneath and the white counterpane pulled smoothly over the top, showing every hump. I showed Mr. Holcombe the splasher, dotted with ink as usual.

"I'll take it off and soak it in milk," I said. "It's his fountain pen. When the ink doesn't run he shakes it, and—"

"Where's the clock?" said Mr. Holcombe, stopping in front of the mantel with his notebook in his hand.

"The clock?"

I turned and looked. My onyx clock was gone from the mantelshelf.

Perhaps it seems strange, but from the moment I missed that clock my rage at Mr. Ladley increased to a fury. It was all I had had left of my former gentility. When times were hard and I got behind with the rent, as happened now and then, more than once I'd been tempted to sell the clock, or to pawn it. But I had never done so. Its ticking had kept me company on many a lonely night, and its elegance had helped me to keep my pride and to retain the respect of my neighbors. For in the flood district onyx clocks are not plentiful. Mrs. Bryan, the saloonkeeper's wife, had one and I had another. That is, I *had* had.

I stood staring at the mark in the dust of the mantelshelf, which Mr. Holcombe was measuring with a pocket tape measure.

"You are sure you didn't take it away yourself, Mrs. Pitman?" he asked.

"Sure? Why, I could hardly lift it," I said.

He was looking carefully at the oblong of dust where the clock had stood. "The key is gone too," he said, busily making entries in his notebook. "What was the maker's name?"

"I don't think I ever noticed."

He turned to me angrily. "Why didn't you notice?" he snapped. "Good God, woman, do you only use your eyes to cry with? How can you wind a clock, time after time, and not know the maker's name? It proves my contention; the average witness is totally unreliable."

"Not at all," I snapped back. "I am ordinarily both accurate and observing."

"Indeed!" he said, putting his hands behind him. "Then perhaps you can tell me the color of the pencil I have been writing with."

"Certainly. Red." Most pencils are red, and I thought this was safe.

But he held out his right hand with a flourish. "I've been writing with a fountain pen," he said in deep disgust, and turned his back on me.

But the next moment he had run to the washstand and pulled it out from the wall. Behind it where it had fallen lay a towel, covered with stains as if someone had wiped bloody hands on it. He held it up, his face working with excitement. I could only cover my eyes.

"This looks better," he said, and began making a quick search of the room, running from one piece of furniture to another, pulling out bureau drawers, drawing the bed out from the wall, and crawling along the baseboard with a lighted match in his hand. He gave a shout of triumph finally, and reappeared from behind the bed with the broken end of my knife in his hand.

"Very clumsy," he said. "*Very* clumsy. Peter the dog could have done better."

I had been examining the wallpaper about the washstand. Among the ink spots were one or two reddish ones that made me shiver. And seeing a scrap of note paper stuck between the baseboard and the wall, I dug it out with a hairpin and threw it into the grate, to be burned later. It was by the merest chance there was no fire there.

The next moment Mr. Holcombe was on his knees by the fireplace reaching for the scrap.

"*Never* do that, under such circumstances," he snapped, fishing among the ashes. "You might throw valuable—Hello, Howell!"

I turned and saw a young man in the doorway, smiling, his hat in his hand. Even at that first glance I liked Mr. Howell, and later, when everyone was against him and many curious things were developing, I stood by him through everything, and even helped him to the thing he wanted more than anything else in the world. But that of course was later.

"What's the trouble, Holcombe?" he asked. "Hitting the trail again?"

"A very curious thing that I just happened on," said Mr. Holcombe. "Mrs. Pitman, this is Mr. Howell, of whom I spoke. Sit down, Howell, and let me read you something."

With the crumpled paper still unopened in his hand, Mr. Holcombe took his notebook and read aloud what he had written. I have it before me now:

"'Dog meat, two dollars, boat hire'—that's not it. Here. 'Yesterday, Sunday, March the 4th, Mrs. Pitman, landlady at 42 Union Street, heard two of her boarders quarreling, a man and his wife. Man's name, Philip Ladley. Wife's name, Jennie Ladley, known as Jennie Brice at the Liberty Stock Company, where she has been playing small parts.'"

Mr. Howell nodded. "I've heard of her," he said. "Not much of an actress, I believe."

"'The husband also was an actor, out of work, and employing his leisure time in writing a play.'"

"Everybody's doing it," said Mr. Howell idly.

"The Shuberts were to star him in this," I put in. "He said that the climax at the end of the second act—"

Mr. Holcombe shut his notebook with a snap. "After we have finished gossiping," he said, "I'll go on."

"'Employing his leisure time in writing a play—'" quoted Mr. Howell.

"Exactly. 'The husband and wife were not on good terms. They quarreled frequently. On Sunday they fought all day, and Mrs.

Ladley told Mrs. Pitman she was married to a fiend. At four o'clock Sunday afternoon, Philip Ladley went out, returning about five. Mrs. Pitman carried their supper to them at six, and both ate heartily. She did not see Mrs. Ladley at the time, but heard her in the next room. They were apparently reconciled. Mrs. Pitman reports Mr. Ladley in high good humor. If the quarrel recommenced during the night the other boarder, named Reynolds, in the next room heard nothing. Mrs. Pitman was up and down until one o'clock, when she dozed off. She heard no unusual sound.

"'At approximately two o'clock in the morning, however, this Reynolds came to her room and said he had heard someone in a boat in the lower hall. He and Mrs. Pitman investigated. The boat which Mrs. Pitman uses during a flood and which she had tied to the stair rail was gone, having been cut loose, not untied. Everything else was quiet, except that Mrs. Ladley's dog had been shut in a third-story room.

"'At a quarter after four that morning Mrs. Pitman, thoroughly awake, heard the boat returning and going to the stairs met Ladley coming in. He muttered something about having gone for medicine for his wife and went to his room, shutting the dog out. This is worth attention, for the dog ordinarily slept in their room.'"

"What sort of dog?" asked Mr. Howell. He had been listening attentively.

"A cocker spaniel. The rest of the night, or early morning, was quiet. At a quarter after seven Ladley asked for coffee and toast for one, and on Mrs. Pitman remarking this, said that his wife was not playing this week and had gone for a few days' vacation, having left early in the morning.' Remember, during the night he had been out for medicine for her. Now she was able to travel, and in fact had already started."

Mr. Howell was frowning at the floor. "If he was doing anything wrong he was doing it very badly," he said.

"This is where I entered the case," said Mr. Holcombe. "I rowed into the lower hall this morning to feed the dog, Peter, who was whining on the staircase. Mrs. Pitman was coming down, pale and agitated over the fact that the dog shortly before had found floating in the parlor downstairs a slipper belonging to Mrs. Ladley, and, later, a knife with a broken blade. She maintains that she had the knife last night upstairs, that it was not broken, and that it was taken from a shelf in her room while she dozed. The question is, then: Why was the knife taken? Who took it? And why? Has this man made away with his wife, or has he not?"

Mr. Howell looked at me and smiled. "Mr. Holcombe and I are old enemies," he said. "Mr. Holcombe believes that circumstantial evidence may probably hang a man. I do not." And to Mr. Holcombe: "So, having found a wet slipper and a broken knife, you are prepared for murder and sudden death!"

"I have more evidence," Mr. Holcombe said eagerly, and proceeded to tell what we had found in the room. Mr. Howell listened, smiling to himself, but at the mention of the onyx clock he got up and went to the mantel.

"By Jove!" he said, and stood looking at the mark in the dust. "Are you sure the clock was here yesterday?"

"I wound it night before last and put the key underneath. Yesterday, before they moved up, I wound it again."

"The key is gone also. Well, what of it, Holcombe? Did he brain her with the clock? Or choke her with the key?"

Mr. Holcombe was looking at his notebook. "To summarize," he said, "we have here as clues indicating a crime the rope, the broken knife, the slipper, the towel, and the clock. Besides, this scrap of paper may contain some information." He opened it and sat gazing at it in his palm. Then, "Is this Ladley's writing?" he asked me in a curious voice.

"Yes."

I glanced at the slip. Mr. Holcombe had just read from his notebook: " 'Rope, knife, slipper, towel, clock.' "

The slip I had found behind the washstand said: "Rope, knife, shoe, towel. Horn—" The rest of the last word was torn off.

Mr. Howell was staring at the mantel. "Clock!" he repeated.

CHAPTER 4

It was after four when Mr. Holcombe had finished going over the room. I offered to make both the gentlemen some tea, for Mr. Pitman had been an Englishman and I had got into the habit of having a cup in the afternoon, with a cracker or a bit of bread. But they refused. Mr. Howell said he had promised to meet a lady, and to bring her through the flooded district in a boat. He shook hands with me and smiled at Mr. Holcombe.

"You will have to restrain his enthusiasm, Mrs. Pitman," he said. "He is a bloodhound on the scent. If his baying gets on your nerves just send for me." He went down the stairs and stepped into the boat. "Remember, Holcombe," he called, "every well-constituted murder has two things, a motive and a corpse. You haven't either, only a mass of piffling details—"

"If everybody waited until he saw flames, instead of relying on the testimony of the smoke," Mr. Holcombe said tartly, "what would the fire loss be?"

Mr. Howell poled his boat to the front door, and sitting down prepared to row out.

"You are warned, Mrs. Pitman," he called to me. "If he doesn't find a body to fit the clues, he's quite capable of making one to fill the demand."

"Horn—" said Mr. Holcombe, looking at the slip again. "The tail of the 'n' is torn off—evidently only part of a word. Hornet, Horning, Horner—Mrs. Pitman, will you go with me to the police station?"

I was more than anxious to go. In fact I could not bear the idea of staying alone in the house, with heaven only knows what concealed in the depths of that muddy flood. I got on my wraps again and Mr. Holcombe rowed me out. Peter plunged into the water to follow, and had to be sent back. He sat on the lower step and whined. Mr. Holcombe threw him another piece of liver, but he did not touch it.

We rowed to the corner of Robinson Street and Federal—it was before Federal Street was raised above the flood level—and left the boat in charge of a boy there. From there we walked to the police station. On the way Mr. Holcombe questioned me closely about the events of the morning, and I recalled the incident of the burned pillow slip. He made a note of it at once, and grew very thoughtful.

He left me at the police station, however. "I'd rather not appear in this, Mrs. Pitman," he said apologetically, "and I think better along my own lines. Not that I have anything against the police. They've done some splendid work. But this case takes imagination, and the police department deals with facts. We have no facts yet. What we need, of course, is to have the man detained until we are sure of our case."

He lifted his hat and turned away, and I went slowly up the steps to the police station. Living as I had in a neighborhood where the police, like the poor, are always with us, and where the visit of the patrol car is one of those familiar sights which no amount of repetition enabled any of us to treat with contempt, I was uncomfortable until I remembered that my grandfather had been one of the first mayors of the city. And that, if the police had been at my house more than once, the entire neighborhood would testify that my boarders were usually orderly.

At the door someone touched me on the arm. It was Mr. Holcombe again.

"I have been thinking it over," he said, "and I believe you'd better not mention the piece of paper you found behind the washstand. They might say the whole thing is a hoax."

"Very well," I agreed, and went in.

The police sergeant in charge knew me at once, having stopped at my house more than once in floodtime for a cup of hot coffee.

"Sit down, Mrs. Pitman," he said. "I suppose you are still making the best coffee and doughnuts in the city of Allegheny? Well, what's the trouble in your district? Want an injunction against the river for trespass?"

"The river has brought me a good bit of trouble," I said. "I'm worried, Mr. Sergeant. I think a woman from my house has been murdered, but I don't know."

"Murdered," he said, and drew up his chair. "Tell me about it."

I told him everything, while he sat back with his eyes half closed and his fingers beating a tattoo on the arm of his chair.

When I finished he got up and went into an inner room. He came back in a moment.

"I want you to come in and tell that to the chief," he said, and led the way.

All told, I repeated my story three times that afternoon, to the sergeant, to the chief of police, and the third time to both of them and two detectives.

The second time the chief made notes of what I said.

"Know this man Ladley?" he asked the others. None of them did, but they all knew of Jennie Brice, and some of them had seen her in the theater.

"Get the theater, Tom," the chief said to one of the detectives.

Luckily, what he learned over the telephone from the theater corroborated my story. Jennie Brice was not in the cast that week, but should have reported that morning (Monday) to rehearse the next week's play. No message had been received from her, and a substitute had been put in her place.

The chief hung up the receiver and turned to me. "You are sure about the clock, Mrs. Pitman?" he asked. "It was there when they moved upstairs to the room?"

"Yes, sir."

"You're certain you will not find it on the parlor mantel when the water goes down?"

"The mantels are uncovered now. It's not there."

"You think Ladley has gone for good?"

"Yes, sir."

"He'd be a fool to try to run away, unless—Graves, you'd better get hold of the fellow, and keep him until either the woman or a body is found. The river is falling. In a couple of days we'll know if she is around the premises anywhere."

Before I left I described Jennie Brice for them carefully. Asked what she probably wore, if she had gone away as her husband said, I had no idea. She had a lot of clothes, and dressed very well. But I recalled that I had seen, lying on the bed, the black and white dress with the red collar. And they took that down, as well as the brown valise.

The chief rose and opened the door for me himself. "If she actually left town at the time you mention," he said, "she ought not to be hard to find. There are not many trains before seven in the morning, and most of them are locals."

"And if she did not, if he—Do you think she is in the house—or the cellar?"

"Not unless Ladley is more of a fool than I think he is," he said, smiling. "Personally, I believe she has gone away, as he says she did. But if she hasn't, he probably took the body with him when he said he was getting medicine, and dropped it in the current somewhere. But we must go slow with all this. There's no use shouting 'wolf' yet."

"But—the towel?"

"He may have cut himself shaving. It *has* been done."

"And the knife?"

He shrugged his shoulders good-naturedly.

"I've seen a perfectly good knife spoiled opening a bottle of pickles."

"But the slipper? And the clock?"

"My good woman, enough shoes and slippers are forgotten in the bottoms of cupboards year after year in floodtime, and are found floating around the streets, to make all the old-clothes men in town happy. I have seen almost everything floating about during one of these annual floods."

"I dare say you never saw an onyx clock floating around," I replied a little sharply. I had no sense of humor that day. He stopped smiling at once and stood tugging at his mustache.

"No," he admitted. "An onyx clock sinks, that's true. That's a very nice point, that onyx clock. He may be trying to sell it, or perhaps—" He did not finish.

I went back immediately, only stopping at the market to get meat for Mr. Reynolds's supper. It was after half past five and dusk was coming on. I got a boat and was rowed directly home. Peter was not at the foot of the steps. I paid the boatman and let him go, and turned to go up the stairs. Someone was speaking in the hall above.

I have read somewhere that no two voices are exactly alike, just as no two violins ever produce precisely the same sound. I think it is what they call the timbre that is different. I have for instance never heard a voice like Mr. Pitman's, although Mr. Harry Lauder's in a phonograph resembles it. And voices have always done for me what odors do for some people, revived forgotten scenes and old memories. But the memory the voice at the head of the stairs brought back was not very old, although I had forgotten it. I seemed to hear again all at once the lapping of the water Sunday morning as it began to come in over the doorsill, the sound of Terry ripping up the parlor carpet, and Mrs. Ladley calling me a she-devil in the next room in reply to this very voice.

But when I got to the top of the stairs it was only Mr. Howell, who had brought his visitor to the flood district, and on getting her splashed with muddy water had brought her to my house for a towel and a cake of soap.

I lighted the lamp in the hall, and Mr. Howell introduced the girl. She was a pretty girl, slim and young, and she had taken her wetting good-naturedly.

"I know we are intruders, Mrs. Pitman," she said, holding out her hand. "Especially now, when you're in trouble."

"I have told Miss Harvey a little," Mr. Howell said, "and I promised to show her Peter, but he's not here."

I think I had known it was my sister's child from the moment I lighted the lamp. There was something of Alma in her, not Alma's hardness or haughtiness but Alma's dark-blue eyes with black lashes and Alma's nose. Alma was always the beauty of the family. What with the day's excitement, and seeing Alma's child like this in my house, I felt things going round and clutched at the stair rail. Mr. Howell caught me.

"Why, Mrs. Pitman!" he said. "What's the matter?"

I got myself in hand in a moment and smiled at the girl.

"Nothing at all," I said. "Indigestion, most likely. Too much tea the last day or two, and not enough solid food. I've been too anxious to eat."

Lida—for she was that to me at once, although I had never seen her before—Lida was all sympathy and sweetness. She actually asked me to go with her to a restaurant and have a real dinner. I could imagine Alma, had she known! But I excused myself.

"I have to cook something for Mr. Reynolds," I said, "and I'm better now anyhow, thank you. Mr. Howell, may I speak to you for a moment?"

He followed me along the back hall, which was dusk.

"I have remembered something I had forgotten, Mr. Howell," I said. "On Sunday morning the Ladleys had a visitor."

"Yes?"

"They had very few visitors."

"I see."

"I did not see him, but I heard his voice." Mr. Howell did not move, but I fancied he drew his breath in quickly. "It sounded—it was not by any chance *you?*"

"I? A newspaperman who goes to bed at three A.M. on Sunday morning, up and about at ten!"

"I didn't say what time it was," I said sharply.

But at that moment Lida called from the front hall.

"I think I hear Peter," she said. "He is shut in somewhere, whining."

We went forward at once. She was right. Peter was scratching at the door of Mr. Ladley's room, although I had left the door closed and Peter in the hall. I let him out and he crawled to me on three legs, whimpering. Mr. Howell bent over him and felt the fourth.

"Poor little beast!" he said. "His leg is broken!"

He made a splint for the dog, and with Lida helping they put him to bed in a clothes basket in my upstairs kitchen. It was easy to see how things lay with Mr. Howell. He was all eyes for her. He made excuses to touch her hand or her arm, little caressing touches that made her color heighten. And with it all there was a sort of hopelessness in his manner, as if he knew how far the girl was out of his reach. Knowing Alma and her pride, I knew better than they how hopeless it was.

I was not so sure about Lida. I wondered if she was in love with the boy, or only in love with love. She was very young, as I had been. God help her, if as I had, she sacrificed everything to discover too late that she was only in love with love.

CHAPTER 5

Mr. Reynolds did not come home to dinner after all. The water had got into the basement at the store, he telephoned, one of the floodgates in a sewer having leaked, and they were moving some of the departments to an upper floor. I had expected to have him in the house that evening, and now I was left alone again.

But as it happened I was not alone. Mr. Graves, one of the city detectives, came at half past six and went carefully over the Ladleys' room. I showed him the towel and the slipper and the broken knife, and where we had found the blade. He was noncommittal, and left in a half hour taking the articles with him in a newspaper.

At seven the doorbell rang. I went down as far as I could on the staircase, and I saw a boat outside the front door, with the boatman and a woman in it. I called to them to bring the boat back along the hall, and I had a queer feeling that it might be Mrs. Ladley and that I'd been making a fool of myself all day for nothing. But it was not Mrs. Ladley.

"Is this number forty-two?" asked the woman, as the boat came back.

"Yes."

"Does Mr. Ladley live here?"

"Yes. But he is not here now."

"Are you Mrs. Pittock?"

"Pitman, yes."

The boat bumped against the stairs, and the woman got out. She was as tall as Mrs. Ladley, and when I saw her in the light from the upper hall I knew her instantly. It was Temple Hope, the leading woman from the Liberty Theater.

"I would like to talk to you, Mrs. Pitman," she said. "Where can we go?"

I led the way back to my room, and when she had followed me in she turned and shut the door.

"Now then," she said without any preliminary, "where is Jennie Brice?"

"I don't know, Miss Hope," I answered.

We looked at each other for a minute, and each of us saw what the other suspected.

"He's killed her!" she exclaimed. "She was afraid he would do it, and he has."

"Killed her and thrown her into the river," I said. "That's what I think, and he'll go free at that. It seems there isn't any murder when there isn't any corpse."

"Nonsense! If he has done that, the river will give her up, eventually."

"The river doesn't always give them up," I retorted. "Not in floodtime anyhow. Or when they are found it is months later, and you can't prove anything."

She had only a little time, being due at the theater soon, but she sat down and told me the story she told afterward on the stand.

She had known Jennie Brice for years, they having been together in the chorus as long before as *Nadjy*.

"She was married then to a fellow on the vaudeville circuit," Miss Hope said. "He left her about that time, and she took up with Ladley. I don't think they were ever married."

"What!" I said, jumping to my feet. "And they came to a respectable house like this! There's never been a breath of scandal about this house, Miss Hope, and if this comes out I'm ruined."

"Well, perhaps they were married," she said. "Anyhow, they were always quarreling. And when he wasn't playing it was worse. She used to come to my hotel and cry her eyes out."

"I knew you were friends," I said. "Almost the last thing she said to me was about the black and white dress of hers you were to borrow for the piece this week."

"Black and white dress? I borrow one of Jennie Brice's dresses!" exclaimed Miss Hope. "I should think not. I have plenty of my own."

That puzzled me, for she had said it, that was sure. And then I remembered I had not seen the dress in the room that day, and I went in to look for it. It was gone. I came back and told Miss Hope.

"A black and white dress! Did it have a red collar?" she asked.

"Yes."

"Then I remember it. She wore a small black hat with a red quill with that dress. You might look for the hat."

She followed me back to the room and stood in the doorway while I searched. The hat was gone too.

"Perhaps after all he's telling the truth," she said thoughtfully. "Her fur coat isn't in the closet, is it?"

It was gone too. It is strange that all day I had never thought of looking over her clothes and seeing what was missing. I hadn't known all she had, of course, but I had seen her all winter in her fur coat and admired it. It was a striped fur, brown and gray, and very unusual. But with the coat missing and a dress and hat gone it began to look as if I had been making a fool of myself, and stirring up a tempest in a teacup. Miss Hope was as puzzled as I was.

"Anyhow, if he didn't kill her," she said, "it isn't because he didn't want to. Only last week she had hysterics in my dressing room and said he threatened to poison her. It was all Mr. Bronson, the business manager, and I could do to quiet her."

She looked at her watch and exclaimed that she was late and would have to hurry. I saw her down to her boat. The river had been falling rapidly for the last hour or two, and I heard the boat scrape as it went over the door sill. I did not know whether to be glad that the water was going down and I could live like a Christian again or to be sorry for fear of what we might find in the mud that was always left.

Peter was lying where I had put him, on a folded blanket laid in a clothes basket. I went back to him and sat down beside the basket.

"Peter!" I said. "Poor old Peter! Who did this to you? Who hurt you?" He looked at me and whined, as if he wanted to tell me if only he could.

"Was it Mr. Ladley?" I asked, and the poor thing cowered close to his bed and shivered. I wondered if it had been he, and if it had why he had come back. Perhaps he had remembered the towel. Perhaps he would come again and spend the night there. I was like Peter. I cowered and shivered at the very thought.

At nine o'clock I heard a boat at the door. It had stuck there, and its occupant was scolding furiously at the boatman. Soon after I heard splashing, and I knew that whoever it was was wading back to the stairs through the foot and a half or so of water still in the hall. I ran back to my room and locked myself in, and then stood armed with the stove-lid lifter, in case it should be Ladley and he should break the door in.

The steps came up the stairs, and Peter barked furiously. It seemed to me that this was to be my end, killed like a rat in a trap and thrown out the window, to float like my kitchen chair into Mollie Maguire's kitchen, or to be found lying in the ooze of the yard after the river had gone down.

The steps hesitated at the top of the stairs, and turned back along the hall. Peter redoubled his noise; he never barked for Mr. Reynolds or the Ladleys. I stood still, hardly able to breathe. The door was thin, and the lock loose. One good blow, and—

The door knob turned, and I screamed. I recall that the light turned black, and that is all I *do* remember until I came to a half hour later, and saw Mr. Holcombe stooping over me. The door, with the lock broken, was standing open.

I tried to move, and then I saw that my feet were propped up on the edge of Peter's basket.

"Better leave them up," Mr. Holcombe said. "It sends the blood back to the head. Half the damfool people in the world stick a pillow under a fainting woman's shoulders. How are you now?"

"All right," I said feebly. "I thought you were Mr. Ladley."

He helped me up, and I sat in a chair and tried to keep my lips from shaking. And then I saw that Mr. Holcombe had brought a suitcase with him, and had set it inside the door.

"You're safe from him, until he gets bail anyhow," he said. "They picked him up as he was boarding a Pennsylvania train bound east."

"For murder?" I asked.

"As a suspicious character," he replied grimly. "That does as well as anything for a time." He sat down opposite me, and looked at me intently.

"Mrs. Pitman," he said, "did you ever hear the story of the horse that wandered out of a village and could not be found?"

I shook my head.

"Well, the best wit of the village failed to locate the horse. But one day the village idiot walked into town leading the missing animal by the bridle. When they asked him how he had done it, he said: 'Well, I just thought what I'd do if I was a horse, and then I went and did it.'"

"I see," I said, humoring him.

"You *don't* see. Now, what are we trying to do?"

"We're trying to find a body. Do you intend to become a corpse?"

He leaned over and tapped on the table between us. "We are trying to prove a crime, and I intend for the time to be the criminal."

He looked so curious, bent forward and glaring at me from under his bushy eyebrows, and with his shoes on his knee—he had taken them off to wade to the stairs—and his trousers rolled up, that I wondered if he was entirely sane. But Mr. Holcombe, eccentric as he might be, was sane enough.

"Not really a criminal?" I asked feebly.

"As really as lies in me. Listen, Mrs. Pitman. I want to put myself in Ladley's place for a day or two, live as he lived, do what he did, even think as he thought if I can. I am going to sleep in his room tonight, with your permission."

I could not see any reason for objecting, although I thought it silly and useless. I led the way to the front room, Mr. Holcombe following with his shoes and suitcase. I lighted a lamp, and he stood looking around him.

"I see you have been here since we left this afternoon," he said.

"Twice," I replied. "First with Mr. Graves, and later—"

The words died on my tongue. Someone had been in the room since my last visit there.

"He has been here!" I gasped. "I left the room in tolerable order. Look at it!"

"When were you here last?"

"At seven-thirty, or thereabouts."

"Where were you between seven-thirty and eight-thirty?"

"In the kitchen with Peter." I told him then about the dog, and about finding him shut in the room.

The washstand was pulled out. The sheets of Mr. Ladley's manuscript, usually an orderly pile, were half on the floor. The bed coverings had been jerked off and flung over the back of a chair.

Peter, imprisoned, might have moved the washstand and upset the manuscript. But Peter had never put the bedclothes over the chair, or broken his own leg.

"Humph!" he said, and getting out his notebook he made an exact memorandum of what I had told him, and of the condition of the room. That done, he turned to me.

"Mrs. Pitman," he said, "I'll thank you to call me Mr. Ladley for the next day or so. I am an actor out of employment, forty-one years of age, short, stout, and bald, married to a woman I would like to be quit of, and I am writing myself a play in which the Shuberts intend to star me, or in which I intend the Shuberts to star me."

"Very well, Mr. Ladley," I said, trying to enter into the spirit of the thing and, God knows, seeing no humor in it. "Then you'll like your soda from the icebox?"

"Soda? For what?"

"For your whisky and soda, before you go to bed, sir."

"Oh, certainly, yes. Bring the soda. And—just a moment, Mrs. Pitman. Mr. Holcombe is a total abstainer, and has always been so. It is Ladley, not Holcombe, who takes this abominable stuff."

I said I quite understood, but that Mr. Ladley could skip a night if he so wished. But the little gentleman would not hear to it, and when I brought the soda he poured himself a double portion. He stood looking at it with his face screwed up, as if the very odor revolted him.

"The chances are," he said, "that Ladley—that I—having a nasty piece of work to do during the night would—will take a larger drink than usual." He raised the glass, only to put it down. "Don't forget," he said, "to put a large knife where you left the one last night. I'm sorry the water has gone down, but I shall imagine it still at the seventh step. Good night, Mrs. Pitman."

"Good night, Mr. Ladley," I said, smiling, "and remember, you are three weeks in arrears with your rent."

His eyes twinkled through his spectacles. "I shall imagine it paid," he said.

I went out, and I heard him close the door behind me. Then through the door I heard a great sputtering and coughing, and I knew he had got the whisky down somehow. I put the knife out, as he had asked me to, and went to bed. I was ready to drop. Not even the knowledge that an imaginary Mr. Ladley was about to commit an imaginary crime in the house that night could keep me awake.

Mr. Reynolds came in at eleven o'clock. I was roused when he banged his door. That was all I knew until morning. The sun on my face wakened me. Peter, in his basket, lifted his head as I moved, and thumped his tail against his pillow in greeting. I put on a wrapper, and called Mr. Reynolds by knocking at his door. Then I went on to the front room. The door was closed, and someone beyond was groaning. My heart stood still, and then raced on. I opened the door and looked in.

Mr. Holcombe was on the bed, fully dressed. He had a wet towel tied around his head, and his face looked swollen and puffy. He opened one eye and looked at me.

"What a night!" he groaned.

"What happened! What did you find?"

He groaned again. "Find!" he said. "Nothing, except that there was something wrong with that whisky. It poisoned me. I haven't been out of the house!"

So for that day at least Mr. Ladley became Mr. Holcombe again, and as such accepted ice in quantities, a mustard plaster over his stomach, and considerable nursing. By evening he was better, but although he clearly intended to stay on he said nothing about changing his identity again, and I was glad enough. The very name of Ladley was horrible to me.

The river went down almost entirely that day, although there was still considerable water in the cellars. It takes time to get rid of that. The lower floors showed nothing suspicious. The papers were ruined, of course, the doors warped and sprung, and the floors coated with mud and debris. Terry came in the afternoon, and together we hung the dining-room rug out to dry in the sun.

As I was coming in I looked over at the Maguire yard. Molly Maguire was there, and all her children around her, gaping. Molly was hanging out a sodden fur coat that had once been striped, brown and gray.

I went over after breakfast and claimed the coat as belonging to Mrs. Ladley. But she refused to give it up. There is a sort of unwritten law concerning the salvage of flood articles, and I had to leave the coat, as I had my kitchen chair. But it was Mrs. Ladley's, beyond a doubt.

I shuddered when I thought how it had probably got into the water. And yet it was curious too, for if she had had it on how did it get loose to go floating around Molly Maguire's yard? And if she had not worn it, how did it get in the water?

CHAPTER 6

The newspapers from that time on were full of the Ladley case, with its curious solution and many surprises. It was considered unique in many ways. Mr. Pitman had always read all the murder trials, and used to talk about the *corpus delicti* and writs of *habeas corpus, corpus* being the legal way, I believe, of spelling corpse. But I came out of the Ladley trial—for it came to trial ultimately—with only one point of law that I was sure of: that was, that it is mighty hard to prove a man a murderer unless you can show what he killed.

And that was the weakness in the Ladley case. There was a body, but it could not be identified.

The police held Mr. Ladley for a day or two and then, nothing appearing, they let him go. Mr. Holcombe, who was still occupying the second-floor front, almost wept with rage and despair when he read the news in the papers. He was still working on the case in his curious way, wandering along the wharves at night, and writing letters all over the country to learn about Philip Ladley's previous life and his wife's. But he did not seem to get anywhere.

The press all over the country had been full of the Jennie Brice disappearance. For disappearance it proved to be. So far as could be learned she had not left the city that night or since, and as she was a striking-looking woman, very blonde, as I have said, with a full voice and a languid manner, she could hardly have taken refuge anywhere without being discovered. The morning after her disappearance a young woman, tall like Jennie Brice and fair, had been seen in the Union Station. But as she was accompanied by a young man who bought her magazines and papers and bade her an excited farewell, sending his love to various members of a family, and promising to feed the canary, this was not seriously considered. A sort of general alarm went over the country. When she was younger she had been pretty well known at the Broadway theaters in New York. One way or another, the Liberty Theater got a lot of free advertising from the case, and I believe Miss Hope's salary was raised.

The police communicated with Jennie Brice's people. She had a sister in Olean, New York, but she had not heard from her. The sister wrote, I heard later, that Jennie had been unhappy with Philip Ladley and afraid he would kill her. And Miss Hope told the same story. But there was no *corpus,* as the lawyers say, and finally the police had to free Mr. Ladley.

Beyond making an attempt to get bail, and failing, he had done nothing. Asked about his wife, he merely shrugged his shoulders and said she had left him and would turn up all right. He was unconcerned, smoked cigarettes all day, ate and slept well, and looked better since he had had nothing to drink. And two or three days after the arrest he sent for the manuscript of his play.

Mr. Howell came for it on the Thursday of that week.

I was on my knees scrubbing the parlor floor when he rang the bell. I let him in, and it seemed to me that he looked tired and pale.

"Well, Mrs. Pitman," he said, smiling, "what did you find in the cellar when the water went down?"

"I'm glad to say that I didn't find what I feared, Mr. Howell."

"Not even the onyx clock?"

"Not even the clock," I replied. "And I feel as if I'd lost a friend. A clock is a lot of company."

"Do you know what I think?" he said, looking at me closely. "I think you put that clock away yourself in the excitement and have forgotten all about it."

"Nonsense"

"Think hard." He was very much in earnest. "You knew the water was rising and the Ladleys would have to be moved up to the second-floor front, where the clock stood. You went in there and looked around to see if the room was ready, and you saw the clock.

And knowing that the Ladleys quarreled now and then, and were apt to throw things—"

"Nothing but a soap dish, and that only once."

"—you took the clock to the attic and put it, say, in an old trunk."

"I did nothing of the sort. I went in, as you say, and I put up an old splasher because of the way he throws ink about. Then I wound the clock, put the key under it, and went out."

"And the key is gone too!" he said thoughtfully. "I wish I could find that clock, Mrs. Pitman."

"So do I."

"Ladley went out Sunday afternoon about three, didn't he, and got back at five?"

I turned and looked at him. "Yes, Mr. Howell," I said. "Perhaps *you* know something about that."

"I?" He changed color. Twenty years of dunning boarders has made me pretty sharp at reading faces, and he looked as uncomfortable as if he owed me money. "I!" I knew then that I had been right about the voice. It had been his.

"You!" I retorted. "You were here Sunday morning and spent some time with the Ladleys. I'm the old she-devil. I notice you didn't tell your friend Mr. Holcombe about having been here on Sunday."

He was quick to recover. "I'll tell you all about it, Mrs. Pitman," he said smilingly. "You see, all my life I have wanted an onyx clock. It has been my ambition, my Great Desire. Leaving the house that Sunday morning and hearing the ticking of the clock, I recognized that it was an onyx clock, clambered from my boat through an upper window and so reached it. The clock showed fight, but after stunning it with a chair—"

"Exactly!" I said. "Then the thing Mrs. Ladley said she would not do was probably to wind the clock?"

He dropped his bantering manner at once. "Mrs. Pitman," he said, "I don't know what you heard or did not hear. But I want you to give me a little time before you tell anybody that I was here that Sunday morning. And in return I'll find your clock."

I hesitated, but however put out he was he didn't look like a criminal. Besides he was a friend of my niece's, and blood is thicker even than flood-water.

"There was nothing wrong about my being here," he went on, "but I don't want it known. Don't spoil a good story, Mrs. Pitman."

I did not quite understand that, although those who followed the trial carefully may do so. Poor Mr. Howell! I am sure he believed that it was only a good story. He got the description of my onyx clock and wrote it down, and I gave him the manuscript for Mr. Ladley. That was the last I saw of him for some time.

That Thursday proved to be an exciting day. Late in the afternoon Terry, digging the mud out of the cellar, came across my missing gray false front near the coal vault and brought it up, grinning. And just before six Mr. Graves, the detective, rang the bell and then let himself in. I found him in the lower hall looking around.

"Well, Mrs. Pitman," he said, "has our friend come back yet?"

"She was no friend of mine."

"Not she. Ladley. He'll be out this evening, and he'll probably be around for his clothes."

I felt my knees waver, as they always did when he was spoken of.

"He may want to stay here," said Mr. Graves. "In fact, I think that's just what he will want."

"Not here," I protested. "The very thought of him makes me quake."

"If he comes here, better take him in. I want to know where he is."

I tried to say that I wouldn't have him, but the old habit of the ward asserted itself. From taking a bottle of beer or a slice of pie to telling one where one might or might not live, the police were autocrats in that neighborhood. And respectable woman that I am, my neighbors' fears of the front office have infected me.

"All right, Mr. Graves," I said.

He pushed the parlor door open and looked in, whistling. "This is the place, isn't it?"

"Yes. But it was upstairs that he—"

"I know. Tall woman, Mrs. Ladley?"

"Tall and blonde. Very airy in her manner."

He nodded and still stood looking in and whistling. "Never heard her speak of a town named Horner, did you?"

"Horner? No."

"I see." He turned and wandered out again into the hall, still whistling. At the door he stopped and turned, however. "Look anything like this?" he asked, and held out one of his hands, with a small kodak picture on the palm.

It was a snapshot of a children's frolic in a village street, with some onlookers in the background. Around one of the heads had been drawn a circle in pencil. I took it to the gas jet and looked at it closely. It was a tall woman with a hat on, not unlike Jennie Brice. She was looking over the crowd, and I could see only her face, and that in shadow. I shook my head.

"I thought not," he said. "We have a lot of stage pictures of her, but what with false hair and their being retouched beyond recognition they don't amount to much." He started out, and stopped on the doorstep to light a cigar.

"Take him on if he comes," he said. "And keep your eyes open. Feed him well and he won't kill you!"

I had plenty to think of when I was cooking Mr. Reynolds's supper: the chance that I might have Mr. Ladley again, and the woman at Horner. For it had come to me like a flash as Mr. Graves left that the "Horn—" on the paper slip might have been "Horner."

CHAPTER 7

After all there was nothing sensational about Mr. Ladley's return. He came at eight o'clock that night, fresh-shaved and with his hair cut, and, although he had a latchkey he rang the doorbell. I knew his ring, and I thought it no harm to carry an old razor of Mr. Pitman's with the blade open and folded back on the handle, the way the colored people use them, in my left hand.

But I saw at once that he meant no mischief.

"Good evening," he said, and put out his hand. I jumped back, until I saw there was nothing in it and that he only meant to shake hands. I didn't do it. I might have to take him in and make his bed and cook his meals, but I did not have to shake hands with him.

"You too!" he said, looking at me with what I suppose he meant to be a reproachful look. But he could no more put an expression of that sort in his eyes than a fish could. "I suppose, then, there is no use asking if I may have my old room? The front room. I won't need two."

I didn't want him, and he must have seen it. But I took him. "You may have it, as far as I'm concerned," I said. "But you'll have to let the paper-hanger in tomorrow."

"Assuredly." He came into the hall and stood looking around him, and I fancied he drew a breath of relief. "It isn't much yet," he said, "but it's better to look at than six feet of muddy water."

"Or than stone walls," I said.

He looked at me and smiled. "Or than stone walls," he repeated, and went into his room.

So I had him again, and if I gave him only the dull knives and locked up the bread knife the moment I had finished with it, who can blame me? I took all the precaution I could think of, had Terry put an extra bolt on every door, and hid the rat poison and the carbolic acid in the cellar.

Peter would not go near him. He hobbled around on his three legs, with the splint beating a sort of tattoo on the floor, but he stayed back in the kitchen with me, or in the yard.

It was Sunday night or early Monday morning that Jennie Brice disappeared. On Thursday evening her husband came back. On Friday the body of a woman was washed ashore at Beaver, down the Ohio River, but turned out to be that of a stewardess who had fallen overboard from one of the Cincinnati packets. Mr. Ladley himself showed me the article in the morning paper when I took in his breakfast.

"Public hysteria has killed a man before this," he said, when I had read it. "Suppose that woman had been mangled, or the screw of the steamer had cut her head off! How many people do you suppose would have been willing to swear that it was my—was Mrs. Ladley?"

"Even without a head I'd know Mrs. Ladley," I retorted.

He shrugged his shoulders. "Let's trust she's still alive, for my sake," he said. "But I'm glad anyhow that this woman has a head. You'll allow me to be glad, won't you?"

"You can be anything you want, as far as I'm concerned," I snapped, and went out.

Mr. Holcombe still retained the second-story front room. I think, although he said nothing more about it, that he was still "playing horse." He wrote a good bit at the washstand, and, from the loose sheets of manuscript he left I believe actually tried to begin a play. But mostly he wandered along the water front or stood on one or another of the bridges, looking at the water and thinking. It is certain that he tried to keep in the part by smoking cigarettes, but he hated them and usually ended by throwing the cigarette away and lighting an old pipe he carried.

On that Thursday evening he came home and sat down to supper with Mr. Reynolds. He ate little and seemed much excited. The talk ran on crime, as it always did when he was around, and Mr. Holcombe quoted Spencer a great deal, Herbert Spencer. Mr. Reynolds was impressed, not knowing much beyond silks and the National League.

"Spencer," Mr. Holcombe would say, "Spencer shows that every occurrence is the inevitable result of what has gone before, and carries in its train an equally inevitable series of results. Try to interrupt this chain in the smallest degree, and what follows? Chaos, my dear sir, chaos."

"We see that at the store," Mr. Reynolds would say. "Accustom a lot of women to a silk sale on Fridays and then make it toothbrushes. That's chaos, all right."

Well, Mr. Holcombe came in that night about ten o'clock and I told him Ladley was back. He was almost wild with excitement, wanted to have the back parlor so he could watch him through the keyhole, and was terribly upset when I told him there was no keyhole, that the door fastened with a thumb bolt. On learning that the room was to be papered the next morning he grew calmer, however, and got the paperhanger's address from me. He went out just after that.

Friday, as I say, was very quiet. Mr. Ladley moved to the back parlor to let the paperhanger in the front room, smoked and fussed with his papers all day, and Mr. Holcombe stayed in his room, which was unusual. In the afternoon Molly Maguire put on the striped fur coat and walked slowly past the house so that I would be sure to see her. Beyond slamming the window I gave her no satisfaction.

At four o'clock Mr. Holcombe came to my kitchen, rubbing his hands together. He had a pasteboard tube in his hand about a foot long, with an arrangement of small mirrors in it. He said it was modeled after the periscope that is used on a submarine, and that he and the paperhanger had fixed a place for it between his floor and the ceiling of Mr. Ladley's room, so that the chandelier would hide it from below. He thought he could watch Mr. Ladley through it; and as it turned out, he could.

"I want to find his weak moment," he said excitedly. "I want to know what he does when the door is closed and he can take off his mask. And I want to know if he sleeps with a light."

"If he does," I replied, "I hope you'll let me know, Mr. Holcombe. The gas bills are a horror to me as it is. I think he kept it on last night. I turned off all the other lights and went to the cellar. The meter was going around."

"Fine!" he said. "Every murderer fears the dark. And our friend of the parlor bedroom is a murderer, Mrs. Pitman. Whether he hangs or not he's a murderer."

The periscope was installed that day and worked amazingly well. Plaster is always falling in those old houses, especially after a flood. Mr. Holcombe had cut a hole in the floor boards of his room upstairs, and the paperhanger had done so in the ceiling below. It was not noticeable from below, having a paper flap which stayed pretty well in place until it was pushed down. It all seemed rather silly to me, but I went into Mr. Holcombe's room with him to try it out, and I distinctly saw the paperhanger take a cigarette from Mr. Ladley's box and put it in his pocket. Just after that Mr. Ladley sauntered into the room and looked at the new paper. I could both see and hear him. It was rather weird.

"God, what a wallpaper!" he said.

He did not look at the ceiling at all.

CHAPTER 8

That was Friday afternoon. All that evening, and most of Saturday and Sunday, Mr. Holcombe sat on the floor with his eye to the reflecting mirror and his notebook beside him. I have it before me.

On the first page is the "dog meat—two dollars" entry. On the next, the description of what occurred on Sunday night, March fourth, and Monday morning the fifth. Following that came a copy, made with a carbon sheet, of the torn paper found behind the washstand:

And then came the entries for Friday, Saturday, and Sunday. Friday evening:

6:30—Eating hearty supper, brought from delicatessen.

7:00—Lights cigarette and paces floor. Notice that when Mrs. P. knocks he goes to desk and pretends to be writing.

8:00—Is examining book. Looks like a railway guide.

8:30—It is a steamship guide.

8:45—Tailor's boy brings box. Gives boy fifty cents. Query: Where does he get money, now that J.B. is gone?

9:00—Tries on new suit, brown.

9:30—Has been spending a quarter of an hour on his knees looking behind furniture and examining baseboard.

10:00—He has the key to the onyx clock. Has hidden it twice, once up the chimney flue, once behind baseboard.

10:15—He has just thrown key or similar small article out window into yard.

11:00—Has gone to bed. Light burning. Shall sleep here on floor.

11:30—He cannot sleep. Is up walking the floor and smoking.

2:00 A.M.—Saturday. Disturbance below. He had had nightmare and was calling "Jennie!" He got up, took a drink, and is now reading.

8:00 A.M.—Must have slept. He is shaving.

12:00 M.—Nothing this morning. He wrote for four hours, sometimes reading aloud what he had written.

2:00 P.M.—He has a visitor, a man. Cannot hear all, only a word now and then. "Llewellyn is the very man." "Devil of a risk—" "We'll see you through." "Lost the slip—"

Then more clearly: "Didn't go to the hotel. She went to a private house." "Eliza Shaeffer."

Who went to a private house? Jennie Brice?

2:30—Cannot hear at all. Are whispering. The visitor has given Ladley roll of bills.

4:00—Followed the visitor, a tall man with a pointed beard. He went to the Liberty Theater. Found it was Bronson, business manager there. Who is Llewellyn, and who is Eliza Shaeffer?

4:15—Had Mrs. P. bring telephone book. Six Llewellyns in the book, no Eliza Shaeffer. Ladley appears more cheerful since Bronson's visit. He has bought all the evening papers and is searching for something. Has not found it.

7:00—Ate well again. Have asked Mrs. P. to take my place here while I interview the six Llewellyns.

11:00—Mrs. P. reports a quiet evening. He read and smoked. Has gone to bed. Light burning. Saw five Llewellyns. None of them knew Bronson or Ladley. Sixth—a lawyer—out at revival meeting. Went to the church and walked home with him. He knows something. Acknowledged he knew Bronson. Had met Ladley. Did not believe Mrs. Ladley dead. Regretted I had not been to the meeting. Good sermon. Asked me for a dollar for missions.

9:00 A.M.—Sunday. Ladley in bad shape. Apparently been drinking all night. Cannot eat. Sent out early for papers and has searched them all. Found entry on second page, stared at it, then flung the paper away. Have sent out for same paper.

10:00 A.M.—Paper says: "Body of woman washed ashore yesterday at Sewickley. Much mutilated by flood debris." Ladley in bed, staring at ceiling. Wonder if he sees tube? He is ghastly.

That is the last entry in the notebook for that day: Mr. Holcombe called me in great excitement shortly after ten and showed me the item. Neither of us doubted for a moment that it was Jennie Brice who had been found. He started for Sewickley that same afternoon, and he probably communicated with the police before he left. For once or twice I saw Mr. Graves, the detective, sauntering past the house.

Mr. Ladley ate no dinner. He went out at four, and I had Mr. Reynolds follow him. But they were both back in a half hour. Mr. Reynolds reported that Mr. Ladley had bought some headache tablets and some bromide powders to make him sleep.

Mr. Holcombe came back that evening. He thought the body was that of Jennie Brice, but the head was gone. He was much depressed, and did not immediately go back to the periscope. I asked if the head had been cut off or taken off by a steamer. He was afraid the latter, as a hand was gone too.

It was about eleven o'clock that night that the doorbell rang. It was Mr. Graves, with a small man behind him. I knew the man; he lived in a shanty-boat not far from my house, a curious affair with shelves full of dishes and tinware. In the spring he would be towed up the Monongahela a hundred miles or so and float down, tying up at different landings and selling his wares. Timothy Senft was his name. We called him Tim.

Mr. Graves motioned me to be quiet. Both of us knew that behind the parlor door Ladley was probably listening.

"Sorry to get you up, Mrs. Pitman," said Mr. Graves, "but this man says he has bought beer here today. That won't do, Mrs. Pitman."

"Beer! I haven't such a thing in the house. Come in and look," I snapped. And the two of them went back to the kitchen.

"Now," said Mr. Graves, when I had shut the door, "where's the dog's-meat man?"

"Upstairs."

"Bring him quietly."

I got Mr. Holcombe and he came eagerly, notebook and all. "Ah!" he said, when he saw Tim. "So you've turned up!"

"Yes, sir."

"It seems, Mr. Dog's—Mr. Holcombe," said Mr. Graves, "that you are right, partly anyhow. Tim here did help a man with a boat that night—"

"Threw him a rope, sir," Tim broke in. "He'd got out in the current, and what with the ice and his not knowing much about a boat he'd have kept on to New Orleans if I hadn't caught him, or to Kingdom Come."

"Exactly. And what time did you say this was?"

"Between three and four last Sunday night, or Monday morning. He said he couldn't sleep and went out in a boat, meaning to keep in close to shore. But he got drawn out in the current."

"Where did you see him first?"

"By the Ninth Street bridge."

"Did you hail him?"

"He saw my light and hailed me. I was making fast to a coal barge after one of my ropes had busted."

"You threw the line to him there?"

"No, sir. He tried to work in to shore. I ran along River Avenue to below the Sixth Street bridge. He got pretty close in there and I threw him a rope. He was about done up."

"Would you know him again?"

"Yes, sir. He gave me five dollars, and said to say nothing about it. He didn't want anybody to know he had been such a fool."

They took him quietly upstairs then and let him look through the periscope. He identified Mr. Ladley absolutely.

When Tim and Mr. Graves had gone, Mr. Holcombe and I were left alone in the kitchen. Mr. Holcombe leaned over and patted Peter as he lay in his basket.

"We've got him, old boy," he said. "The chain *is* just about complete. He'll never kick you again."

But Mr. Holcombe was wrong, not about kicking Peter, although I don't believe Mr. Ladley ever did that again, but in thinking we had him.

I washed that next morning, Monday, but all the time I was rubbing and starching and hanging out my mind was with Jennie Brice. The sight of Molly Maguire, next door, at the window, rubbing and brushing at the fur coat, only made things worse.

At noon when the Maguire youngsters came home from school I bribed Tommy, the youngest, into the kitchen with the promise of a doughnut.

"I see your mother has a new fur coat," I said, with the plate of doughnuts just beyond his reach.

"Yes'm."

"She didn't buy it?"

"Sure she didn't buy it. Say, Mrs. Pitman, gimme that doughnut."

"Oh, so the coat washed in?"

"No'm. Pop found it down by the Point, on a cake of ice. He thought it was a dog and rowed out for it."

Well, I hadn't wanted the coat, as far as that goes. I'd managed well enough without furs for twenty years or more. But it was a satisfaction to know that it had not floated into Mrs. Maguire's kitchen and spread itself at her feet, as one may say. However, that was not the question, after all. The real issue was that if it was Jennie Brice's coat, and was found across the river on a cake of ice, then one of two things was certain. Either Jennie Brice's body wrapped in the coat had been thrown into the water, out in the current, or she herself, hoping to incriminate her husband, had flung her coat into the river.

I told Mr. Holcombe, and he interviewed Joe Maguire that afternoon. The upshot of it was that Tommy had been correctly informed. Joe had witnesses who had lined up to see him rescue a dog, and had beheld his return in triumph with a wet and soggy fur coat. At three o'clock Mrs. Maguire, instructed by Mr. Graves, brought the coat to me for identification, turning it about for my inspection but refusing to take her hands off it.

"If her husband says to me that he wants it back, well and good," she said, "but I don't give it up to nobody but him. Some folks I know of would be glad enough to have it."

I was certain it was Jennie Brice's coat, but the maker's name had been ripped out. With Molly holding one arm and I the other, we took it to Mr. Ladley's door and knocked. He opened it, grumbling.

"I have asked you not to interrupt me," he said, with his pen in his hand. Then his eyes fell on the coat. "What's that?" he asked, changing color.

"I think it's Mrs. Ladley's fur coat," I said.

He stood there looking at it and thinking. Then: "It can't be hers," he said. "She wore hers when she went away."

"Perhaps she dropped it in the water."

He looked at me and smiled. "And why would she do that?" he asked mockingly. "Was it out of fashion?"

"That's Mrs. Ladley's coat," I persisted, but Molly Maguire jerked it from me and started away. He stood there looking at me and smiling in his nasty way.

"This excitement is telling on you, Mrs. Pitman," he said coolly. "You're too emotional for detective work." Then he went in and shut the door.

When I went downstairs Molly Maguire was waiting in the kitchen, and had the audacity to ask me if I thought the coat needed a new lining!

It was on Monday evening that the strangest event in years happened to me. I went to my sister's house! And the fact that I was admitted at a side entrance made it even stranger. It happened in this way:

Supper was over, and I was cleaning up, when an automobile came to the door. It was Alma's car. The chauffeur gave me a note:

Dear Mrs. Pitman—I am not at all well, and very anxious. Will you come to see me at once? My mother is out to dinner and I am alone. The car will bring you.

Cordially,

Lida Harvey.

I put on my best dress at once and got into the limousine. Half the neighborhood was out watching. I leaned back in the upholstered seat, fairly quivering with excitement. This was Alma's car. That was Alma's cardcase. The little clock had her monogram on it. Everything about it reminded me of Alma, a trifle showy but good to look at. And I was going to her house!

I was not taken to the main entrance, but to a side door. The queer dreamlike feeling was still there. In this back hall, separated from the more conspicuous part of the house, there were even pieces of furniture from our old home, and my father's picture in an oval gilt frame hung over my head. I had not seen a picture of him for twenty years. I went over and touched it gently.

"Father, father!" I said.

Under it was the tall hall chair that I had climbed over as a child, and had stood on many times to see myself in the mirror above. The chair was newly finished and looked the better for its age. I glanced in the old glass. The chair had stood time better than I. I was a middle-aged woman, lined with poverty and care, shabby, prematurely gray, a little hard. I had thought father an old man when that picture was taken, and now I was even older. "Father!" I whispered again, and fell to crying in the dimly lighted hall.

Lida sent for me at once. I had only time to dry my eyes and straighten my hat. Had I met Alma on the stairs I would have passed her without a word. She would not have known me. But I saw no one.

Lida was in bed. She was lying there with a rose-shaded lamp beside her and a great bowl of spring flowers on a little stand at her elbow. She sat up when I went in and had a maid place a chair for me beside the bed. She looked very childish, with her hair spread over the pillow and her slim young arms and throat bare.

"I'm so glad you came," she said, and would not be satisfied until the light was just right for my eyes, and my coat unfastened and thrown open.

"I'm not really sick," she informed me. "I'm just tired and nervous and—and unhappy, Mrs. Pitman."

"I'm sorry," I said. I wanted to lean over and pat her hand, to draw the covers around her and mother her a little. I had had no one to mother for so long. But I could not. She would have thought it queer and presumptuous—or, no, not that. She was too sweet to have thought that.

"Mrs. Pitman," she said suddenly, "who was this Jennie Brice?"

"She was an actress. She and her husband lived at my house."

"I never saw her acting: was she—was she beautiful?"

"Well," I said slowly, "I never thought of that. She was handsome, in a large way."

"Was she young?"

"Yes. Twenty-eight or so."

"That isn't very young," she said, looking relieved. "But I don't think men like very young women. Do you?"

"I know one who does," I said, smiling. But she sat up in bed suddenly and looked at me with her clear childish eyes.

"I don't want him to like me," she flashed. "I want him to hate me."

"Tut, tut! You want nothing of the sort."

"Mrs. Pitman," she said, "I sent for you because I'm nearly crazy. Mr. Howell was a friend of that woman. He has acted like a maniac since she disappeared. He doesn't come to see me, he has given up his work on the paper, and I saw him today on the street—he looks like a ghost."

That put me to thinking.

"He might have been a friend," I admitted. "Although, as far as I know, he was never at the house but once, and then he saw both of them."

"When was that?"

"Sunday morning, the day before she disappeared. They were arguing about something."

She was looking at me attentively. "You know more than you are telling me, Mrs. Pitman," she said. "Do you think Jennie Brice is dead, and that Mr. Howell knows who did it?"

"I think she is dead, and I think possibly Mr. Howell suspects who did it. He doesn't know, or he would have told the police."

"You don't think he was in love with her, do you?"

"I'm certain of that," I said. "He is very much in love with a foolish girl, who ought to have more faith in him than she has."

She colored a little and smiled at that, but the next moment she was sitting forward, tense and questioning again.

"If that's true, Mrs. Pitman," she said, "who was the woman he met Monday morning at daylight and took across the bridge to Pittsburgh? I believe it was Jennie Brice. If it wasn't, who was it?"

"I don't believe he took any woman across the bridge at that hour. Who says he did?"

"Uncle Jim saw him. He had been playing cards all night at one of the clubs, and was walking home. He says he met Mr. Howell face to face, and spoke to him. The woman was tall, but he couldn't see her face. Uncle Jim sent for him a day or two later, and he refused to explain. Then they forbade him the house. Mother objected to him anyhow and he only came on sufferance. He's a college man. His family is all right too. But he has no money at all except what he earns. And now—"

I had had some young newspapermen staying with me, and I knew what they got. They were nice boys, but they made about twenty-five dollars a week. I'm afraid I smiled a little as I looked around the room, with its pale-gray walls, its toilet table spread with ivory and gold, and the maid in attendance in her black dress and white apron, collar and cuffs. Even the little nightgown Lida was wearing would have taken a week's salary or more. She saw my smile.

"It was to be his chance," she said. "If he made good he was to have something better. My uncle Jim owns the paper and he promised me to help him. But—"

So Jim was running a newspaper. That was a curious career for Jim to choose. Jim, who was twice expelled from school, and who could never write a letter without a dictionary beside him! I had a pang when I heard his name again, after all the years. For I had written to Jim from Oklahoma after Mr. Pitman died, asking for money to bury him, and had never even had a reply.

"And you haven't seen him since?" I inquired.

"Once. I didn't hear from him, and I called him up. We met in the park. He said everything was all right, but he couldn't tell me anything just then. The next day he resigned from the paper and went away. Mrs. Pitman, it's driving me crazy! For they have found a body and they think it's hers. If it is, and he was with her—"

"Don't be a foolish girl," I protested. "If he was with Jennie Brice, she's still living, and if he was not with Jennie Brice—"

"If it wasn't Jennie Brice, then I have a right to know who it was," she declared. "He was not like himself at all when I met him. He said such queer things. He talked about an onyx clock, and said he had been made a fool of, and that no matter what came out I was always to remember that he had done what he did for the best. And that—that he cared for me more than for anything else in this world or the next."

"That wasn't so foolish." I couldn't help it. I leaned over and drew the blanket up over her bare white shoulder. "You won't help anything or anybody by taking cold, my dear," I said. "Call your maid and have her put a bed jacket on you."

I left soon after. There was little I could do. But I comforted her as best I could, and said good night. My heart was heavy as I went downstairs. For, twist things as I might, it was clear that in some way the Howell boy was mixed up in the Brice case. Poor little troubled Lida! Poor distracted boy!

I had a curious experience downstairs. I had reached the foot of the staircase and was turning to go back along the hall to the side entrance, when I came face to face with Isaac, the old colored man who had driven the family carriage when I was a child, and whom I had seen at intervals since I came back, pottering around Alma's house. The old man was bent and feeble. He came slowly down the hall with a bunch of keys in his hand. I had seen him do the same thing many times.

He stopped when he saw me and I shrank back from the light, but he had seen me. "Miss Bess!" he said. "Foh Gawd's sake, Miss Bess!"

"You are making a mistake, my friend," I said, quivering. "I am not Miss Bess!"

He came close to me and stared into my face. And from that he looked at my cloth gloves, at my old coat, and he shook his white head. "I sure thought you was Miss Bess," he said, and made no further effort to detain me. He led the way back to the door where the car waited, his head shaking with the palsy of age, and muttering as he went. He opened the door with his best manner, and stood aside.

"Good night, ma'am," he quavered.

I had tears in my eyes. I tried to keep them back. "Good night," I said. "Good night, *Ikkie.*"

It had slipped out, my baby name for old Isaac.

"Miss Bess!" he cried. "Oh, praise Gawd, it's Miss Bess again!"

He caught my arm and pulled me back into the hall, and there he held me, crying over me, muttering praises for my return, begging me to come back, recalling little tender things out of the past which almost killed me to hear again.

But I had made my bed and must lie in it. I forced him to swear silence about my visit. I made him promise not to reveal my identity to Lida, and I told him—Heaven forgive me—that I was well and prosperous and happy.

Dear old Isaac! I would not let him come to see me, but the next day there came a basket with six bottles of wine, and an old daguerreotype of my mother which had been his great treasure. Nor was that basket the last.

Perhaps he followed me home that night. Certainly he discovered where I lived.

CHAPTER 9

The coroner held an inquest over the headless body the next day,
Tuesday. Mr. Graves telephoned me in the morning, and I went to
the morgue with him.

I do not like the morgue, although some of my neighbors pay it
weekly visits. It is by way of excursion, like the nickelodeons or
watching the circus put up its tents. I have heard them threaten the
children that if they misbehaved they would not be taken to the
morgue that week.

But I failed to identify the body. How could I? It had been a tall
woman, probably five feet eight, and I thought the nails looked like
those of Jennie Brice. The thumbnail of one was broken short off,
and I told Mr. Graves about her speaking of a broken nail. But he
shrugged his shoulders and said nothing.

There was a curious scar over the heart, and he was making a
sketch of it. It reached from the center of the chest for about six
inches across the left breast, a narrow thin line that one could hardly
see. It was shaped like this:

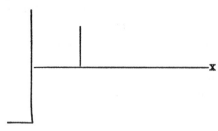

I felt sure that Jennie Brice had had no such scar, and Mr. Graves thought as I did. Temple Hope, called to the inquest, said she had never heard of one, and Mr. Ladley himself at the inquest swore that his wife had had nothing of the sort. I was watching him, and I did not think he was lying. Yet the hand was very like Jennie Brice's. It was all bewildering.

Mr. Ladley's testimony at the inquest was disappointing. He was cool and collected, said he had no reason to believe that his wife was dead and less reason to think she had been drowned. She had left him in a rage, and if she found out that by hiding she was putting him in an unpleasant position she would probably hide indefinitely.

To the disappointment of everybody the identity of the woman remained a mystery. No one with such a scar was missing. A small woman of my own age, a Mrs. Murray whose daughter, a stenographer, had disappeared, attended the inquest. But her daughter had had no such scar, and had worn her nails short because of using the typewriter. Alice Murray was the missing girl's name. Her mother sat beside me, and cried most of the time.

One thing was brought out at the inquest. The body had been thrown into the river after death. There was no water in the lungs. The verdict was "death at the hands of some person or persons unknown."

Mr. Holcombe was not satisfied. In some way or other he had got permission to attend the autopsy, and had brought away a tracing of the scar. All the way home in the streetcar he stared at the drawing, holding first one eye shut and then the other. But, like the coroner, he got nowhere. He folded the paper and put it in his notebook.

"None the less, Mrs. Pitman," he said, "that is the body of Jennie Brice. Her husband killed her, probably by strangling her. He took the body out in the boat and dropped it into the swollen river above the Ninth Street bridge."

"Why do you think he strangled her?"

"There was no mark on the body, and no poison was found."

"Then if he strangled her, where did the blood in the room come from?"

"I didn't limit myself to strangulation," he said irritably. "He may have cut her throat."

"Or brained her with my onyx clock," I added, with a sigh. For I missed the clock more and more.

He went down in his pockets and brought up a key. "I'd forgotten this," he said. "It shows you were right, that the clock was there when the Ladleys took the room. I found this in the yard this morning."

It was when I got home from the inquest that I found old Isaac's basket waiting. I am not a crying woman, but I could hardly see my mother's picture for tears. Well, after all, that is not the Brice story. I am not writing the sordid tragedy of my life.

That was on Tuesday. Jennie Brice had been missing nine days. In all that time, although she was cast for the piece at the theater that week, no one there had heard from her. Her relatives had had no word. She had gone away, if she had gone, on a cold March night in a striped black and white dress with a red collar and a red and black hat, but without her fur coat, which she had worn all winter. She had gone very early in the morning, or during the night. How had she gone? Mr. Ladley said he had rowed her to Federal Street at half after six and had brought the boat back. After they had quarreled violently all night, and when she was leaving him, wouldn't he have allowed her to take herself away? Besides, the police had found no trace of her on any early train. And then at daylight, between five and six, my own brother had seen a woman with young Howell, a woman who might have been Jennie Brice. But if it was, why did Mr. Howell not say so?

Mr. Ladley claimed she was hiding, to make trouble for him. But Jennie Brice was not that sort of woman. There was something big about her, something which is found often in large women, a lack of spite. She was not petty or malicious. Her faults, like her virtues, were for all to see.

In spite of the failure to identify the body Mr. Ladley was arrested that night, Tuesday, and this time it was for murder. I know now that the police were taking long chances. They had no strong motive for the crime. As Mr. Holcombe said, they had provocation but not motive, which is different. They had opportunity, and they had a lot of straggling links of clues, which in the total made a fair chain of circumstantial evidence. But that was all.

That is the way the case stood on Tuesday night, March the thirteenth.

Mr. Ladley was taken away at nine o'clock. He was perfectly cool, asked me to help him pack a suitcase, and whistling while it was being done. He requested to be allowed to walk to the jail, and went quietly, with a detective on one side and I think a sheriff's officer on the other.

Just before he left, he asked for a word or two with me, and when he paid his bill up to date and gave me an extra dollar for taking care of Peter I was almost overcome. He took the manuscript of his play with him, and I remember his asking if he could have any typing done in the jail. I had never seen a man arrested for murder before, but I think he was probably the coolest suspect the officers had ever seen. They hardly knew what to make of it.

Mr. Reynolds and I had a cup of tea after all the excitement, and were sitting at the dining-room table drinking it when the bell rang. It was Mr. Howell. He half staggered into the hall when I opened the door, and was for going into the parlor bedroom without a word.

"Mr. Ladley's gone, if you want him," I said. I thought his face cleared.

"Gone!" he said. "Where?"

"To jail."

He did not reply at once. He stood there, tapping the palm of one hand with the forefinger of the other. He was dirty and unshaved. His clothes looked as if he had been sleeping in them.

"So they've got him!" he muttered finally, and turning was about to go out the front door without another word. But I caught his arm.

"You're sick, Mr. Howell," I said. "You'd better not go out just yet."

"Oh, I'm all right." He took his handkerchief out and wiped his face. I saw that his hands were shaking.

"Come back and have a cup of tea and a slice of homemade bread."

He hesitated and looked at his watch. "I'll do it, Mrs. Pitman," he said. "I suppose I'd better throw a little fuel into this engine of mine. It's been going hard for several days."

He ate like a wolf. I cut half a loaf into slices for him, and he drank the rest of the tea. Mr. Reynolds creaked up to bed and left him still eating, and me still cutting and spreading. Now that I had a chance to see him, I was shocked. The rims of his eyes were red, his collar was dirty, and his hair hung over his forehead. But when he finally sat back and looked at me his color was better.

"So they've canned him!" he said.

"High time, too," said I.

He leaned forward and put both his elbows on the table. "Mrs. Pitman," he said earnestly, "I don't like him any more than you do. But he never killed that woman."

"Somebody killed her."

"How do you know? How do you know she's dead?"

Well, I didn't, of course. I only felt it.

"The police haven't even proved a crime. They can't hold a man for a supposititious murder."

"Perhaps they can't but they're doing it," I retorted. "If the woman's alive she won't let him hang."

"I'm not so sure of that," he said heavily, and got up. He looked in the little mirror over the sideboard and brushed back his hair. "I look bad enough," he said, "but I feel worse. Well, you've saved my life, Mrs. Pitman. Thank you."

"How is my—how is Miss Harvey?" I asked, as we started out. He turned and smiled at me in his boyish way.

"The best ever!" he said. "I haven't seen her for days, and it seems like centuries. She's the only girl in the world for me, Mrs. Pitman, although I—" He stopped and drew a long breath. "She is beautiful, isn't she?"

"Very beautiful," I answered. "Her mother was always—"

"Her mother!" He looked at me curiously.

"I knew her mother years ago," I said, putting the best face on my mistake that I could.

"Then I'll remember you to her, if she ever allows me to see her again. Just now I'm *persona non grata*."

"If you'll do the kindly thing, Mr. Howell," I said, "you'll forget me to her."

He looked into my eyes and then thrust out his hand.

"All right," he said. "I'll not ask any questions. I guess there are some curious stories hidden in these old houses."

Peter hobbled to the front door with him. He had not gone as far as the parlor once while Mr. Ladley was in the house.

They had had a sale of spring flowers at the store that day, and Mr. Reynolds had brought me a pot of white tulips. That night I hung my mother's picture over the mantel in the dining room, and put the tulips beneath it. It gave me a feeling of comfort; I had never seen my mother's grave, or put flowers on it.

CHAPTER 10

I have said before that I do not know anything about the law. I believe that the Ladley case was unusual in several ways. Mr. Ladley had once been well known in New York among the people who frequent the theaters, and Jennie Brice was even better known. A good many lawyers, I believe, said that the police had not a leg to stand on, and I know the case was watched with much interest by the legal profession. People wrote letters to the newspapers, protesting against Mr. Ladley's being held. And I believe that the district attorney, in taking him before the grand jury, hardly hoped to secure an indictment.

But he did, to his own surprise, I fancy, and the trial was set for May. In the meantime, however, many curious things had happened.

In the first place, the week following Mr. Ladley's arrest my rooms were filled up with eight or ten members of a touring company from the Gaiety Theater, very cheerful and jolly and well behaved. Three men, I think, and the rest girls. One of the men was named John Bellows, and it turned out that he had known Jennie Brice very well.

From the moment he learned this Mr. Holcombe hardly left him. He walked to the theater with him and waited to walk home again. He took him out to restaurants and for long walks or rides in the mornings, and on the last night of their stay, Saturday, they got gloriously drunk together—Mr. Holcombe, no doubt, in his character of Ladley—and came reeling in at three in the morning, singing. Mr. Holcombe was very sick the next day, but by Monday he was all right, and he called me into the room.

"We've got him, Mrs. Pitman," he said, looking mottled but cheerful. "As sure as God made little fishes we've got him." That was all he would say. It seemed he was going to New York, and might be gone for a month. "I've no family," he said, "and enough money to keep me. If I find my relaxation in hunting down criminals, it's a harmless and cheap amusement, and it's my own business."

He went away that night, and I must admit I missed him. I rented the parlor bedroom the next day to a schoolteacher, and I found the periscope affair very handy. I could see just how much gas she used, and although the notice on each door forbids cooking and washing in rooms, I found she was doing both: making coffee and boiling an egg in the morning, and rubbing out stockings and handkerchiefs in her washbowl. I'd much rather have men as boarders than women. The women are always lighting alcohol lamps on the bureau, and wanting the bed turned into a cozy corner so they can see their gentlemen friends in their rooms.

Well, with Mr. Holcombe gone, and Mr. Reynolds busy all day and half the night getting out the summer silks and preparing for remnant day, and with Mr. Ladley in jail and Lida out of the city— for I saw in the papers that she was not well, and her mother had taken her to Bermuda—I had a good bit of time on my hands. And so I got in the habit of thinking things over and trying to draw conclusions, as I had seen Mr. Holcombe do. I would sit down and write things out as they had happened, and study them, and especially I worried over how we could have found a slip of paper in Mr. Ladley's room with a list, almost exact, of the things we had discovered there.

I used to read it over, "rope, knife, shoe, towel, Horn—" and get more and more bewildered. "Horn-might have been a town, or it might not have been. There was a town called Horner, according to Mr. Graves, but apparently he had made nothing of it. Was it a town that was meant?

The dictionary gave only a few words beginning with "horn"— hornet, hornblende, hornpipe, and horny, none of which was of any assistance. And then one morning I happened to see in the

personal column of one of the newspapers that a woman named
Eliza Shaeffer of Horner had day-old Buff Orpington and Plymouth
Rock chicks for sale, and it started me to puzzling again. Perhaps it
had been Horner, and possibly this very Eliza Shaeffer—

I suppose my lack of experience was in my favor, for, after all,
Eliza Shaeffer is a common enough name, and the "Horn" might
have stood for hornswoggle for all I knew. The story of the man
who thought of what he would do if he were a horse came back to
me, and for an hour or so I tried to think I was Jennie Brice, wanting to get away and hide from my rascal of a husband. But I made
no headway. I would never have gone to Horner, or to any small
town, if I had wanted to hide. I think I should have gone around
the corner and taken a room in my own neighborhood, or have
lost myself in some large city.

It was that same day that, since I did not go to Horner, Horner
came to me. The bell rang about three o'clock, and I answered it
myself. For with times hard and only two or three roomers all
winter I had not had a servant, except Terry to do odd jobs, for
some months.

There stood a fresh-faced young girl holding a covered basket.

"Are you Mrs. Pitman?" she asked.

"I don't need anything today," I said, trying to shut the door.
And at that minute something in the basket cheeped. Young women
selling poultry are not common in our neighborhood. "What have
you there?" I asked more agreeably.

"Chicks, day-old chicks, but I'm not trying to sell you any. I—
may I come in?"

It was dawning on me then that perhaps this was Eliza Shaeffer.
I led her back to the dining room, with Peter sniffing at the basket.

"My name is Shaeffer," she said. "I've seen your name in the
papers, and I believe I know something about Jennie Brice."

Eliza Shaeffer's story was curious. She said that she was postmis-
tress at Horner, and lived with her mother on a farm a mile out of
the town, driving in and out each day in a buggy.

On Monday afternoon, March fifth, a woman had alighted at the
station from a train and had eaten lunch at the hotel. She told the

clerk she was on the road selling corsets, and was much disappointed to find no store of any size in the town. The woman, who had registered as Mrs. Jane Bellows, said she was tired and would like to rest for a day or two on a farm. She was told to see Eliza Shaeffer at the post office and, as a result, drove out with her to the farm after the last mail came in that evening.

Asked to describe her, the girl said she was over medium height, light-haired, quick in her movements, and wore a black and white striped dress with a red collar and hat to match. She carried a small brown valise which Miss Shaeffer presumed contained her samples.

Mrs. Shaeffer had made her welcome, although they did not usually take boarders until June. She had not eaten much supper, and that night she had asked for pen and ink and had written a let-ter. The letter was not mailed until Wednesday. All of Tuesday Mrs. Bellows had spent in her room, and Mrs. Shaeffer had driven to the village in the afternoon with word that she had been crying all day, and bought some headache medicine for her.

On Wednesday morning, however, she had appeared at breakfast, eaten heartily, and had asked Miss Shaeffer to take her letter to the post office. It was addressed to Mr. Ellis Howell, in care of a Pittsburgh newspaper.

That night when Miss Eliza went home, about half past eight, the woman was gone. She had paid for her room and had been driven as far as Thornville, where all trace of her had been lost. On account of the disappearance of Jennie Brice being published shortly after that, Eliza and her mother had driven to Thornville, but the station agent there was surly. They had learned nothing about the woman.

Since that time, three men had made inquiries about the woman in question. One had a Vandyke beard. The second from the description I fancied must have been Mr. Graves. The third with-out doubt was young Howell. Eliza Shaeffer said that this last man had seemed half frantic. I brought her photographs of Jennie Brice in a couple of plays. She said there was a resemblance, but that it ended there. Only of course, as Mr. Graves had said, by the time an actress gets her photograph retouched to suit her it doesn't particularly resemble her. And unless I had known Jennie Brice myself I should hardly have recognized the pictures.

Well, in spite of all that, there seemed no doubt that Jennie Brice had been living three days after her disappearance, and that would clear Mr. Ladley. But what had Mr. Howell to do with it all? Why had he not told the police of the letter from Horner? Or about the woman on the bridge? Why had Mr. Bronson, who was likely the man with the pointed beard, said nothing about having traced Jennie Brice to Horner?

I did as I thought Mr. Holcombe would have wished me to do. I wrote down on a clean sheet of note paper all that Eliza Shaeffer said, the description of the black and white dress, the woman's height, and the rest. Then I took her to the courthouse, chicks and all, and she told her story there to one of the assistant district attorneys.

The young man was interested, but not convinced. He had her story taken down, and she signed it. He was smiling as he bowed us out. I turned in the doorway.

"This will free Mr. Ladley, I suppose?" I asked.

"Not just yet," he said pleasantly. "This makes just eleven places where Jennie Brice spent the first three days after her death."

"But I can positively identify the dress."

"My good woman, that dress has been described, to the last stilted arch and colonial volute, in every newspaper in the United States!"

That evening the newspapers announced that during a conference at the jail between Mr. Ladley and James Bronson, business manager at the Liberty Theater, Mr. Ladley had attacked Mr. Bronson with a chair and almost brained him.

CHAPTER 11

Eliza Shaeffer went back to Horner, after delivering her chicks somewhere in the city, and things went on as before. The trial was set for May. The district attorney's office had all the material we had found in the house that Monday afternoon, the stained towel, the broken knife and its blade, the slipper that had been floating in the parlor, and the rope that had fastened my boat to the staircase. Somewhere—wherever they keep such things—was the headless body of a woman with a hand missing and with a curious scar across the left breast. The slip of paper which I had found behind the baseboard, however, was still in Mr. Holcombe's possession, nor had he mentioned it to the police.

Mr. Holcombe had not come back. He wrote me twice asking me to hold his room, once from New York and once from Chicago. To the second letter he added a postscript:

> Have not found what I wanted, but am getting warm. If any news, address me at Des Moines, Iowa, General Delivery.
> H.

It was nearly the end of April when I saw Lida again. I had seen by the newspapers that she and her mother were coming home. I wondered if she had heard from young Howell, for I had not, and I wondered too if she would send for me again.

But she came herself, on foot, late one afternoon, and the school-teacher being out I took her into the parlor bedroom. She looked thinner than before and rather white. My heart ached for her.

"I've been away," she explained. "I thought you might wonder why you didn't hear from me. But, you see, my mother—" She stopped and flushed. "I would have written you from Bermuda, but my mother watched my correspondence, so I couldn't."

No. I knew she couldn't. Alma had once found a letter of mine to Mr. Pitman. Very little escaped Alma.

"I wondered if you have heard anything?" she asked.

"I have heard nothing. Mr. Howell was here once, just after I saw you. I didn't believe he is in the city."

"Perhaps not, although—Mrs. Pitman, I believe he is in the city, hiding."

"Hiding? Why?"

"I don't know. But last night I thought I saw him below my window. I opened the window, so if he was there, he could see me. But he moved on without a word. Later whoever it was came back. I put out my light and watched. Someone stood there in the shadow until after two this morning. Part of the time he was looking up."

"Don't you think, had it been Howell, he would have spoken when he saw you?"

She shook her head. "He's in trouble," she said. "He hasn't heard from me, and he thinks I don't care any more. Just look at me, Mrs. Pitman! Do I look as if I don't care?"

She looked half killed, poor lamb.

"He may be out of town, searching for a better position," I tried to comfort her. "He wants to have something to offer more than himself."

"I only want him," she said, looking at me frankly. "I don't know why I tell you all this, but you're so kind, and I have to talk to someone."

She sat there, in the cozy corner the schoolteacher had made with a portiere and some cushions, and I saw she was about ready to break down and cry. I went over to her and took her hand, for she was my own niece, although she didn't suspect it, and I had never had a child of my own.

But after all I could not help her much. I could only assure her that he would come back and explain everything, and that he was all right, and that the last time I had seen him he had spoken of her, and had said she was "the best ever." My heart fairly yearned over the girl, and I think she felt it. For she kissed me shyly when she was leaving.

With the newspaper files before me it is not hard to give the details of that sensational trial. It commenced on Monday, the seventh of May, but it was late Wednesday when the jury was finally selected. I was at the courthouse early on Thursday, and so was Mr. Reynolds.

The district attorney made a short speech. "We propose, gentlemen, to prove that the prisoner, Philip Ladley, murdered his wife," he said in part. "We will show first that a crime was committed. Then we will show a motive for this crime. And finally we expect to show that the body washed ashore at Sewickley is the body of the murdered woman, and thus establish beyond doubt the prisoner's guilt."

Mr. Ladley listened with attention. He wore the brown suit, and looked well and cheerful. He was much more like a spectator than a prisoner, and he was not so nervous as I was.

Of that first day I don't recall much. I was called early in the day. The district attorney questioned me.

"Your name?"

"Elizabeth Marie Pitman."

"Your occupation?"

"I keep a boardinghouse at 42 Union Street."

"You know the prisoner?"

"Yes. He was a boarder in my house."

"For how long?"

"From December first. He and his wife came at that time."

"Was his wife the actress, Jennie Brice?"

"Yes, sir."

"Were they living together at your house the night of March fourth?"

"Yes, sir."

"In what part of the house?"

"They rented the double parlors downstairs, but on account of the flood I moved them upstairs to the second-floor front."

"That was on Sunday? You moved them on Sunday?"

"Yes, sir."

"At what time did you retire that night?"

"Not at all. The water was very high. I lay down dressed at one o'clock, and dropped into a doze."

"How long did you sleep?"

"An hour or so. Mr. Reynolds, a boarder, roused me to say he had heard someone rowing a boat in the lower hall."

"Do you keep a boat around during floodtimes?"

"Yes, sir."

"What did you do when Mr. Reynolds roused you?"

"I went to the top of the stairs. My boat was gone."

"Was the boat secured?"

"Yes, sir. By a rope. Anyhow there was no current in the hall."

"What did you do then?"

"I waited a time and went back to my room."

"What examination of the house did you make, if any?"

"Mr. Reynolds looked around."

"What did he find?"

"He found Peter, the Ladleys' dog, shut in a room on the third floor."

"Was there anything unusual about that?"

"I had never known it to happen before."

"State what happened later."

"I did not go to sleep again. At a quarter after four I heard the boat come back. I took a candle and went to the stairs. It was Mr. Ladley. He said he had been out getting medicine for his wife."

"Did you see him tie up the boat?"

"Yes."

"Did you observe any stains on the rope?"

"I did not notice any."

"What was the prisoner's manner at that time?"

"I thought he was surly."

"Now, Mrs. Pitman, tell us about the following morning."

"I saw Mr. Ladley at a quarter before seven. He said to bring breakfast for one. His wife had gone away. I asked if she was not ill and he said no, that she had gone away early, that he had rowed her to Federal Street, and that she would be back Saturday. It was shortly after that when the dog Peter brought in one of Mrs. Ladley's slippers, water-soaked."

"You recognized the slipper?"

"Positively. I had seen it often."

"What did you do with it?"

"I took it to Mr. Ladley."

"What did he say?"

"He said at first that it was not hers. Then he said if it was she would never wear it again. Then he added, because it was ruined."

"Did he offer any statement as to where his wife was?"

"No, sir. Not at that time. Before, he had said she had gone away for a few days."

"Tell the jury about the broken knife."

"The dog found it floating in the parlor with the blade broken off."

"You had not left it downstairs?"

"No, sir. I had used it upstairs the night before, and left it on a mantel of the room I was using as a temporary kitchen."

"Was the door of this room locked?"

"No. It was standing open."

"Were you asleep in this room?"

"Yes. For some hours."

"You heard no one come in?"

"No one until Mr. Reynolds roused me."

"Where did you find the blade?"

"Behind the bed in Mr. Ladley's room."

"What else did you find in the room?"

"A bloodstained towel behind the washstand. Also my onyx clock was missing."

"Where was the clock when the Ladleys were moved up into this room?"

"On the mantel. I wound it just before they came upstairs."

"When you saw Mrs. Ladley on Sunday did she say she was going away?"

"No, sir."

"Did you see any preparation for a journey?"

"The black and white dress was laid out on the bed, and a small bag. She said she was taking the dress to the theater to lend to Miss Hope."

"Is that all she said?"

"No. She said she'd been wishing her husband would drown; that he was a fiend.

I could see that my testimony had made an impression. I tried not to look at Mr. Ladley, but it was difficult. When I did he looked relaxed, and once he even smiled at me. It was all a most unpleasant experience, and it was not over.

CHAPTER 12

The slipper, the rope, the towel, and the knife and blade were produced in court, and I identified them all. They made a noticeable impression on the jury. Then Mr. Llewellyn, the lawyer for the defense, cross-examined me.

"Is it not true, Mrs. Pitman," he said, "that many articles, particularly shoes and slippers, are found floating around during a flood?"

"Yes," I admitted.

"Now, you say the dog found this slipper floating in the hall and brought it to you. Are you sure this slipper belonged to Jennie Brice?"

"She wore it. I presume it belonged to her."

"Ahem. Now, Mrs. Pitman, after the Ladleys had been moved to the upper floor, did you search their bedroom and the connecting room downstairs?"

"No, sir."

"Ah. Then how do you know that this slipper was not left on the floor or in a closet?"

"It is possible, but not likely. Anyhow, it was not the slipper alone. It was the other things *and* the slipper. It was——"

"Exactly. Now, Mrs. Pitman, this knife. Can you identify it positively?"

"I can."

"But isn't it true that this is a very common sort of knife? One that nearly every housewife has in her possession?"

"Yes, sir. But that knife handle has three notches in it. I put the notches there myself."

"Before this presumed crime?"

"Yes, sir."

"For what purpose?"

"My neighbors were constantly borrowing things. It was a means of identification."

"Then this knife is yours?"

"Yes."

"Tell again where you left it the night before it was found floating downstairs."

"On a shelf over the stove."

"Could the dog have reached it there?"

"Not without standing on a hot stove."

"Is it not possible that Mr. Ladley, unable to untie the boat, borrowed your knife to cut the boat's painter?"

"No painter was cut that I heard about. The paperhanger—"

"No, no. The boat's painter—the rope."

"Oh! Well, he might have. He never said."

"Now then, this towel, Mrs. Pitman. Did not the prisoner, on the following day, tell you that he had cut his wrist in freeing the boat, and ask you for some court plaster?"

"He did not," I said firmly.

"You have not seen a scar on his wrist?"

"No." I glanced at Mr. Ladley: he was smiling again, as if amused. It made me angry. "And what's more," I flashed, "if he has a cut on his wrist, he put it there himself, to account for the towel."

I was sorry the next moment that I had said it, but it was too late. The counsel for the defense moved to exclude the answer and I received a caution that I deserved. Then:

"You saw Mr. Ladley when he brought your boat back?"

"Yes."

"What time was that?"

"A quarter after four Monday morning."

"Did he come in quietly, like a man trying to avoid attention?"

"Not particularly. It would have been of no use. The dog was barking."

"What did he say?"

"That he had been out for medicine. That his wife was sick."

"Do you know a pharmacist named Alexander, Jonathan Alexander?"

"There is such a one, but I don't know him."

I was excused, and Mr. Reynolds was called. He had heard no quarreling that Sunday night; had even heard Mrs. Ladley laughing. This was about nine o'clock. Yes, they had fought in the afternoon. He had not overheard any words, but their voices were quarrelsome, and once he heard a chair or some article of furniture overthrown. Was awakened about two by footsteps on the stairs, followed by the sound of oars in the lower hall. He told his story plainly and simply. Under cross-examination admitted that he was fond of detective stories and had tried to write one himself; that he had said at the store that he would like to see that "conceited ass" swing, referring to the prisoner; that he had sent flowers to Jennie Brice at the theater, and had made a few advances to her, without success.

My head was going around. I don't know yet how the police learned it all, but by the time poor Mr. Reynolds left the stand half the people there believed that he had been in love with Jennie Brice, that she had spurned his advances, and that there was more to the story than any of them had suspected.

Miss Hope's story held without any alteration under the cross-examination. She was perfectly at ease, looked handsome and well dressed, and could not be shaken. She told how Jennie Brice had been in fear of her life and had asked her, only the week before she disappeared, to allow her to go home with her—Miss Hope. She told of the attack of hysteria in her dressing room, and that the missing woman had said that her husband would kill her someday. There was much wrangling over her testimony, and I believe at least a part of it was not allowed to go to the jury. But I am not a lawyer, and I repeat what I recall.

"Did she say that he had attacked her?"

"Yes, more than once. She was a large woman, fairly muscular, and had always held her own."

"Did she say that these attacks came when he had been drinking?"

"I believe he was worse then."

"Did she give any reason for her husband's attitude to her?"

"She said he wanted to marry another woman."

There was a small sensation at this. If proved, it established a motive.

"Did she know who the other woman was?"

"I believe not. She was away most of the day, and he put in his time as he liked."

"Did Miss Brice ever mention the nature of the threats he made against her?"

"No, I think not."

"Have you examined the body washed ashore at Sewickley?"

"Yes," in a low voice.

"Is it the body of Jennie Brice?"

"I cannot say."

"Does the remaining hand look like the hand of Jennie Brice?"

"Very much. The nails are filed to points, as she wore hers."

"Did you ever know of Jennie Brice having a scar on her breast?"

"No, but that would be easily concealed."

"Just what do you mean?"

"Many actresses conceal defects. She could have worn flesh-colored plaster and covered it with powder. Also, such a scar would not necessarily be seen."

"Explain that."

"Most of Jennie Brice's décolleté gowns were cut to a point. That would conceal such a scar."

Miss Hope was excused, and Jennie Brice's sister from Olean was called. She was a smaller woman than Jennie Brice had been, very lady-like in her manner. She said she was married and living in Olean. She had not seen her sister for several years, but had heard from her often. The witness had discouraged the marriage to the prisoner.

"Why?"

"She had had bad luck before."

"She had been married before?"

"Yes, to a man named John Bellows. They were in vaudeville together, on the Keith Circuit. They were known as the Pair of Bellows."

I sat up at this, for John Bellows had boarded at my house.

"Mr. Bellows is dead?"

"I think not. She divorced him."

"Did you know of any scar on your sister's body?"

"I never heard of one."

"Have you seen the body found at Sewickley?"

"Yes," faintly.

"Can you identify it?"

"No, sir."

A flurry was caused during the afternoon by Timothy Senft. He testified to what I already knew, that between three and four on Monday morning, during the height of the flood, he had seen from his shanty-boat a small skiff caught in the current near the Ninth Street bridge. He had shouted encouragingly to the man in the boat, running out a way on the ice to make him hear. He had told him to row with the current, and to try to steer in toward shore. He had followed close to the riverbank in his own boat. Below Sixth Street the other boat was within rope-throwing distance. He had pulled it in, and had towed it well back out of the current. The man in the boat was the prisoner. Asked if the prisoner gave any explanation—yes, he said he couldn't sleep, and had thought to tire himself rowing. He had been caught in the current before he knew it. He himself saw nothing suspicious in or about the boat. As they passed the police patrol boat, the prisoner had called to ask if there was much distress, and expressed regret when told there was.

Tim was excused. He had made a profound impression. I would not have given a dollar for Mr. Ladley's chance with the jury, at that time.

CHAPTER 13

The prosecution produced many witnesses during the next two days: Shanty-boat Tim's story withstood the most vigorous cross-examination. After him, Mr. Bronson from the theater corroborated Miss Hope's story of Jennie Brice's attack of hysteria in the dressing room, and told of taking her home that night.

He was a poor witness, nervous and halting. He weighed each word before he said it, and he made a generally unfavorable impression. I thought he was holding something back. In view of what Mr. Pitman would have called the denouement, his attitude is easily explained. But I was puzzled then.

So far the prosecution had touched but lightly on the possible motive for a crime, the other woman. But on the third day, to my surprise, a Mrs. Agnes Murray was called. It was the Mrs. Murray I had seen at the morgue.

I have lost the clipping of that day's trial, but I remember her testimony perfectly.

She was a widow, living above a small millinery shop on Federal Street, Allegheny. She had one daughter, Alice, who did stenography and typing as a means of livelihood. She had no office, and worked at home. Many of the small stores in the neighborhood employed her to send out their bills. There was a card at the street entrance beside the shop, and now and then strangers brought her work.

Early in December the prisoner had brought her the manuscript of a play to type, and from that time on he came frequently, sometimes every day, bringing a few sheets of manuscript at a time.

Sometimes he came without any manuscript, and would sit and talk while he smoked a cigarette. They had thought him unmarried.

On Wednesday, February twenty-eighth, Alice Murray had disappeared. She had taken some of her clothing, not all, and had left a note. The witness read the note aloud in a trembling voice:

Dear Mother: When you get this I shall be married to Mr. Ladley. Don't worry. Will write again from N.Y.

Lovingly,

Alice.

From that time until a week before she had not heard from her daughter. Then she had a card, mailed from Times Square Station, New York City. The card merely said:

Am well and working.   Alice.

The defense was visibly shaken. They had not expected this; and I thought even Mr. Ladley, whose calm had continued unbroken, paled.

So far all had gone well for the prosecution. They had proved a crime, as nearly as circumstantial evidence could prove a crime, and they had established a motive. But in the identification of the body, so far they had failed. The prosecution "rested," as they say, although they didn't rest much, on the afternoon of the third day.

The defense called first of all Eliza Shaeffer. She told of a woman answering the general description of Jennie Brice having spent two days at the Shaeffer farm at Horner. Being shown photographs of Jennie Brice, she said she thought it was the same woman, but was not certain. She told further of the woman leaving unexpectedly on Wednesday of that week from Thornville. On cross-examination, being shown the small photograph which Mr. Graves had shown me, she identified the woman in the group as being the woman in question. As the face was in shadow, she knew it more by the dress and hat: she described the black and white dress and the hat with red trimming.

The defense then called me. I had to admit that the dress and hat as described were almost certainly the ones I had seen on the bed in Jennie Brice's room the day before she disappeared. I could not say definitely whether the woman in the photograph was Jennie Brice or not; but under a magnifying glass I thought it might be.

After that the defense called Jonathan Alexander, the druggist. He testified that on the night in question he had been roused at half past three by the prisoner, who had said his wife was ill, and had purchased a bottle of a proprietary remedy from him. He made an excellent witness, I must say, and his identification was absolute.

After that the defense called Jennie Brice's sister, and endeavored to prove that Jennie Brice had had no such scar. It was shown that she was on intimate terms with her family and would hardly have concealed an operation of any gravity from them.

All in all the defense scored that day. They had shown that the prisoner had told the truth when he said he had gone to a pharmacy for medicine that night for his wife; and they had shown that a woman, answering the description of Jennie Brice, had spent two days in a town called Horner, and had gone from there on the Wednesday after the crime. They had shown too that this woman was dressed exactly as Jennie Brice had been.

And that was the way things stood on the afternoon of the fourth day, when court adjourned.

Mr. Reynolds was at home when I got there. He had been very much subdued since the developments of that first day of the trial, had sat mostly in his own room, and had brought me a bunch of jonquils as a peace offering. He even had the kettle boiling for tea when I got home.

"You have had a number of visitors," he said. "Our young friend Howell has been here, and Mr. Holcombe is back. He has a man in his room. I don't know who it is."

Mr. Holcombe came down a moment after, with his face beaming. He refused tea, and stood looking at me and rubbing his hands together.

"I think we've got him, Mrs. Pitman," he said, almost gaily. "The jury won't even go out of the box."

But further than that he would not explain. He said he had a witness locked in his room, and he'd be glad of supper for him, as they'd both come a long way. After that he went out and bought some oysters and so on and a bottle or two of beer. But as far as I know, he kept his unknown locked up all that night in the second-story front room. I don't think the man realized he was a prisoner. I went in to turn down the bed, and he was sitting by the window, reading the evening paper's account of the trial; an elderly gentleman, rather professional looking.

Mr. Holcombe slept on the upper landing of the hall that night, rolled in a blanket. Not that I think his witness even thought of escaping, but the little man was taking no chances. He was still in a state of excitement, and I doubt if he slept very much.

At eight o'clock that night the doorbell rang. It was Mr. Howell. I admitted him myself, and he followed me back to the dining room. I had not seen him for several weeks, and the change in him startled me. He was dressed carefully, but his eyes were sunk in his head, and he looked as if he had not slept for days.

Mr. Reynolds had gone upstairs, not finding me socially inclined, and I was alone.

"You haven't been sick, Mr. Howell, have you?" I asked.

He did not answer at once. He lit a cigarette and took a turn or two around the room. When he spoke it was as though he had only just realized my question.

"Oh, no," he said. "I'm well enough. I've been traveling about, that's all, and those infernal sleeping cars . . ."

His voice trailed off and I saw him looking at my mother's picture, with the jonquils beneath.

"That's curious!" he said, going closer. "It looks almost like Lida Harvey."

"My mother," I said simply.

"Have you seen her lately?"

"My mother?" I asked, startled.

"No, Lida."

"I saw her a few days ago."

"Here?"

"Yes. She came here, Mr. Howell, two weeks ago. She looks badly, as if she is worrying."

"You mean about me?" he asked eagerly.

"Yes, about you. What on earth possessed you to run away like that? It was idiotic. When my bro—when her uncle accused you of something you simply beat it, instead of facing things like a man."

"I was trying to find the one person who could clear me, Mrs. Pitman." He sat back, with his eyes closed. He looked ill enough to be in bed.

"What happened? Did you succeed?"

"No," he said, his voice bleak.

I thought perhaps he had not been eating and I offered to get him some food, as I had once before. But he refused, with the ghost of his boyish smile.

"I'm hungry, all right, but it's not food I want. I want to see Lida," he said. "I've got to see her, somehow."

I sat down across from him and tried to darn a tablecloth, but I could not sew. I kept seeing those two young things, each sick for a sight of the other, and from wishing they could have a minute together; finally I got to planning it for them.

"Perhaps," I said, "if you want it very much—"

"What do you think?"

"And if you will sit quiet, and stop lighting one cigarette after another until you drive me crazy, I might manage it for you. For five minutes," I said. "Not a second longer."

He came right over and put his arms around me.

"Who are you, anyhow?" he said. "You turn to the world the frozen mask of a Union Street boardinghouse landlady, but you are a gentlewoman by every instinct and training, and a girl at heart. Who are you?"

"I'll tell you what I am," I said. "I'm a romantic old fool, and you'd better let me do this quickly, before I change my mind."

He freed me at that, but he followed to the telephone, and stood by while I got Lida. He was in a perfect frenzy of excitement, flushing with anxiety, and in the middle of the conversation taking the receiver bodily from me and holding it to his own ear.

She said she thought she could get away. She spoke guardedly, as if Alma were near, but I gathered that she would come as soon as she could; and, from the way her voice broke, I knew she was as excited as the boy beside me.

She came, slipping in very quietly, at a quarter after ten that night, and I took her back to the dining room, where he was waiting. He did not make a move toward her, but stood there with his very heart in his eyes, looking at her. And at first she did not make a move either. She stood and stared at him, thin and white as he was, a wreck of himself. Then she made the first gesture.

"Ell darling!" she cried, and ran around the table to him as he held out his arms.

The schoolteacher was out, so I went into the parlor bedroom and sat in her silly cozy corner in the dark. I had done a wrong thing, and I was glad of it. And sitting there in the darkness, I went over my own life again. After all, it had been my own life. I had lived it. No one else had shaped it for me. And if it was cheerless and colorless now it had had its big moments. Life is measured by big moments.

If I let the two children in the dining room have fifteen big moments, instead of five, who can blame me? But I could not let them stay long. There were too many chances of interruption. And I did not yet know his story.

CHAPTER 14

The next day was the sensational one of the trial. We went through every phase of contradiction: Jennie Brice was living. Jennie Brice was dead. The body found at Sewickley could not be Jennie Brice's. The body found at Sewickley was Jennie Brice's. And so it went on.

Then the defense did an unexpected thing in putting Mr. Ladley on the stand. That day for the first time he showed the wear and tear of the ordeal. He had no flower in his buttonhole, and the rims of his eyes were red from strain. But he was quite cool. His stage training had taught him not only to endure the eyes of the crowd, but to find in its gaze a sort of stimulant. He made a good witness, I must admit.

He replied to the usual questions easily. After five minutes or so Mr. Llewellyn got down to work.

"Mr. Ladley, you have said that your wife was ill the night of March fourth?"

"Yes."

"What was the nature of her illness?"

"She had a functional heart trouble, not serious."

"Will you tell us fully the events of that night?"

"I had been asleep when my wife wakened me. She asked for a medicine she used in these attacks. I got up and found the bottle, but it was empty. As she was nervous and frightened, I agreed to try to get some at a drugstore. I went downstairs, took Mrs. Pitman's boat, and went to several stores before I could awaken a pharmacist."

"You cut the boat loose?"

"Yes. It was tied in a woman's knot, or series of knots. I could not untie it, and I was in a hurry."

"How did you cut it?"

"With my pocketknife."

"You did not use Mrs. Pitman's bread knife?"

"I did not."

"And in cutting it you cut your wrist, did you?"

"Yes. The knife slipped. I have the scar still."

"What did you do then?"

"I went back to the room, and wiped off the blood with a towel."

"From whom did you get the medicine?"

"From Alexander's Pharmacy."

"At what time?"

"I am not certain. About three o'clock, probably."

"You went directly back home?"

Mr. Ladley hesitated. "No," he said finally. "My wife had had these attacks, but they were not serious. I was curious to see how the river front looked and rowed out too far. I was caught in the backwash of the flood and carried upstream for some distance."

"You came home after that?"

"Yes, at once. Mrs. Ladley was better and had dropped asleep. She wakened as I came in. She was disagreeable about the length of time I had been gone, and wouldn't let me explain. We quarreled, and she said she was going to leave me. I said that as she had threatened this before and had never done it, I would see that she really started. At daylight I rowed her to Federal Street."

"What did she take with her?"

"A small brown valise."

"How was she dressed?"

"In a black and white dress and hat, with a long black coat."

"What was the last you saw of her?"

"She was going across the Sixth Street bridge."

"Alone?"

"No. She went with a young man we knew."

There was a stir in the courtroom at this.

"Who was this young man?"

"A Mr. Howell, a reporter on a newspaper here."

"Have you seen Mr. Howell since your arrest?"

"No, sir. He has been out of the city."

I was so excited by this time that I could hardly hear. I missed some of the cross-examination. However, I do remember how, when the offense took over, the district attorney pulled Mr. Ladley's testimony to pieces, bit by bit.

"You say you cut the boat's painter with your pocketknife?"

"I did."

"Then how do you account for Mrs. Pitman's broken knife, with the blade found in your room?"

"I have no theory about it. She may have broken it herself. She had used it the day before to lift tacks out of a carpet."

That was true, of course, I had.

"That early Monday morning was cold, was it not?"

"Yes. Very."

"Then why did your wife leave without her fur coat?"

"I didn't know she had until we had left the house. Then I didn't ask her. She wouldn't speak to me."

"I see. But isn't it true that, upon a wet fur coat being shown you as your wife's, you said it could not be hers, as she had taken hers with her?"

"I do not recall such a statement."

"You recall a coat being shown you?"

"Yes. Mrs. Pitman brought a coat to my door, but I was working on a play I am writing, and I do not remember what I said. The coat was ruined. I did not want it. I probably said the first thing I thought of to get rid of the woman."

I got up at that. I'd held my peace about the bread knife, but this was too much. However, the moment I started to speak, somebody pushed me back into my chair and told me to be quiet.

"Now, you say you were in such a hurry to get this medicine for your wife that you cut the rope, thus cutting your wrist."

"Yes. I have the scar still."

"You could not wait to untie the boat, and yet you went along the river front to see how high the water was?"

"Her alarm had excited me. But when I got out, and remembered that the doctors had told us she would never die in an attack, I stopped worrying."

"You got the medicine first, you say?"

"Yes."

"Mr. Alexander has testified that you got the medicine at three-thirty. It has been shown that you left the house at two, and got back about four. Doesn't this show that with all your alarm you went to the river front first?"

"I was gone from two to four," he replied calmly. "Mr. Alexander must be wrong about the time I wakened him. I got the medicine first."

"When your wife left you at the bridge, did she say where she was going?"

"No, sir. She still wouldn't speak to me."

"You claim that this woman at Horner was your wife?"

"I think it likely. It's the sort of thing she would do."

"Was there an onyx clock in the second-story room when you moved into it?"

"I don't recall any clock."

"Your wife didn't take an onyx clock away with her?"

The courtroom tittered, and Mr. Ladley smiled. "No," he said. "Why should she?"

The defense called Mr. Howell next. He looked rested and some-what happier for having seen Lida, but he was still pale, and he showed the strain of some hidden anxiety. What that anxiety was the next two days were to tell us all.

"Mr. Howell," Mr. Llewellyn asked, "you know the prisoner?"

"Slightly."

"State when you met him."

"On Sunday morning, March the fourth. I went to see him."

"Will you tell us the nature of that visit?"

"My paper had heard he was writing a play, intending to star in it himself. I was to get an interview, with photographs if possible."

"You saw his wife at that time?"

"Yes."

"When did you see her again?"

"The following morning, at six o'clock, or a little later. I walked across the Sixth Street bridge with her and put her on a train for Horner, Pennsylvania."

"You are positive it was Mrs. Brice?"

"Yes. I watched her get out of the boat, while her husband steadied it."

"If you knew all this, why didn't you come forward sooner?"

"I've been out of the city."

"But you knew the prisoner had been arrested and that this testimony of yours would be invaluable to him."

"Yes, sir. But I thought it necessary to produce Jennie Brice herself. My unsupported word—"

"You have been searching for Jennie Brice?"

"I have. Since March the eighth."

There was a stir in the courtroom at this, especially when he added that he had not been able to locate her. But the noise subsided as the attorney for the defense went on.

"How was she dressed when you saw her last?"

"She wore a red and black hat and a black coat. She carried a small brown valise."

"Thank you."

The cross-examination that followed did not shake his testimony. But it brought out some curious things. Mr. Howell refused to say how he happened to be at the end of the Sixth Street bridge at that hour, or why he had thought it necessary, on meeting a woman he claimed to have known only twenty-four hours, to go with her to the railway station and put her on a train.

Nevertheless, I could see that the jury was visibly impressed and much shaken. For Mr. Howell carried conviction in every word he said. He looked the district attorney in the eye, and once when our glances crossed he even smiled at me faintly. But I saw why he had tried to find Jennie Brice, and had dreaded testifying. Not a woman in that courtroom, and hardly a man, but believed when he left the stand that he was or had been Jennie Brice's lover. And as such was assisting her to leave her husband.

"Then you believe," the district attorney said at the end, "you believe, Mr. Howell, that Jennie Brice is living?"

"Jennie Brice was living on Monday morning, March the fifth," he said stubbornly.

"Miss Shaeffer has testified that on Wednesday this woman, the one you claim was Jennie Brice, sent a letter to you from Horner. Is that the case?"

"Yes."

"The letter was signed 'Jennie Brice'?"

"It was signed J.B."

"Will you show the court that letter?"

"I destroyed it. There was no reason for keeping it."

"It was a personal letter?"

"It merely said she had arrived safely, and not to let anyone know where she was."

"And yet you destroyed it?"

He hesitated.

"A postscript said to do so," he admitted finally.

"Why?"

"I don't know. An extra precaution probably. She didn't want to be found."

"You were under the impression that she was going to stay there?"

"She was to have remained for a week. So she said anyhow."

"And you have been searching for this woman for two months?"

He looked uncomfortable, but his voice was steady. "Yes," he said. "I wanted no miscarriage of justice."

He was telling the truth, even if it was not all the truth, and I believe had it gone to the jury then Mr. Ladley would have been acquitted. But late that afternoon things took a new turn. Counsel for the prosecution stated to the court that he had a new and important witness, and got permission to introduce this further evidence. The witness was a Doctor Littlefield, and proved to be my one-night tenant of the second-floor front.

Holcombe's prisoner of the night before took the stand. The doctor was less impressive in full daylight; he was a trifle shiny, a

bit bulbous as to nose and indifferent as to fingernails. But his testimony was given with due professional weight.

"You are a doctor of medicine, Doctor Littlefield?" asked the
district attorney.

"Yes, sir."

"In active practice?"

"I have a Cure for Inebriates in Des Moines, Iowa. I was formerly
in general practice in New York City."

"You knew Jennie Ladley?"

"I had seen her at different theaters. And she consulted me pro-
fessionally at one time in New York."

"You operated on her, I believe?"

"Yes. She came to me to have a name removed. It had been tattooed over her heart."

"You removed it?"

"Not at once. I tried fading the marks with goat's milk, but she
was impatient. On the third visit to my office she demanded that
the name be cut out."

"You did it?"

"Yes. She refused a general anesthetic and I used cocaine. The
name was John, I believe of a former husband. She intended to
marry again."

A titter ran over the courtroom. People strained to the utmost
are always glad of an excuse to smile. The laughter of a wrought-up
crowd always seems to me half hysterical.

"Have you seen photographs of the scar on the body found at
Sewickley? Or the body itself?"

"No, sir, I have not."

"Will you describe the operation?"

"I made a transverse incision for the body of the name, and two
vertical ones—one longer for the 'J,' the other shorter for the stem
of the 'h.' There was a dot after the name. I made a half-inch incision for it."

"Will you sketch the cicatrix as you recall it?"

The doctor made a careful drawing on a pad that was passed to
him. The drawing was much like this.

Line for line, dot for dot, it was the scar on the body found at Sewickley.

"You are sure the woman was Jennie Brice?"

"She sent me tickets for the theater shortly after. And I had an announcement of her marriage to the prisoner some weeks later."

"Were there any witnesses to the operation?"

"My assistant. I can produce him at any time."

That was not all of the trial, but it was the decisive moment. Shortly after that the jury withdrew, and for twenty-four hours not a word was heard from them.

CHAPTER 15

After twenty-four hours' deliberation, the jury brought in a verdict of guilty. It was a first-degree verdict. Mr. Howell's unsupported word had lost out against a scar.

Contrary to my expectation Mr. Holcombe was not jubilant over the verdict. He came into the dining room that night and stood by the window, looking out into the yard.

"It isn't logical," he said. "In view of Howell's testimony, it's ridiculous! Heaven help us under this jury system, anyhow! Look at the facts! Howell knows the woman; he sees her on Monday morning, and puts her on a train to go out of town. The boy is telling the truth. He has nothing to gain by coming forward, and everything to lose. Very well. She was alive on Monday. We know where she was on Tuesday and Wednesday. Anyhow, during those days her gem of a husband was in jail. He was freed Thursday night, and from that time until his rearrest on the following Tuesday, I had him under observation every moment. He left the jail Thursday night, and on Saturday the body floated in at Sewickley. If it was done by Ladley it must have been done on Friday, and on Friday he was in view through the periscope all day!"

Mr. Reynolds came in and joined us. "There's only one way out that I see," he said mildly. "Two women have been fool enough to have a name tattooed over their hearts. No woman ever thought enough of me to have *my* name put on her."

"I hope not," I retorted. Mr. Reynolds's first name is Zachariah.

But, as Mr. Holcombe said, all that had been proved was that Jennie Brice was dead, probably murdered. He could not understand

96

the defense letting the case go to the jury without their putting more stress on Mr. Howell's story. But we were to understand that soon, and many other things. Mr. Holcombe told me that evening of learning from John Bellows of the tattooed name on Jennie Brice and of how, after an almost endless search, he had found the man who had cut the name away.

At eight o'clock the doorbell rang. Mr. Reynolds had gone to lodge, he being an Elk and several other things, and much given to regalia put away in boxes, and having his picture in the newspapers in different outlandish costumes. Mr. Pitman used to say that man, being denied his natural love for barbaric adornment in his everyday clothing, took to the different fraternities as an excuse for decking himself out. But this has nothing to do with the doorbell.

It was old Isaac. He had a basket in his hand, and he stepped into the hall and placed it on the floor.

"Evening, Miss Bess," he said. "Can you see a bit of company tonight?"

"I can always see you," I replied. But he had not meant himself. He stepped to the door, and opening it beckoned to someone across the street. It was Lida.

She came in, her color a little heightened, and old Isaac stood back beaming at us both. I believe it was one of the crowning moments of the old man's life, thus to see his Miss Bess and Alma's child together.

"Is—is he here yet?" she asked me nervously.

"I didn't know he was coming." There was no need to ask which "he." There was only one for Lida.

"He telephoned me, and asked me to come here. Oh, Mrs. Pitman, I'm so afraid for him!" She had quite forgotten Isaac. I turned to the schoolteacher's room and opened the door. "The woman who belongs here is out at a lecture," I said. "Come in here, Ikkie, and I'll find the evening paper for you."

"'Ikkie'!" said Lida, and stood staring at me. I think I went white.

"The lady heah and I is old friends," Isaac said, with his splendid manner. "Her mothah, Miss Lida, her mothah—"

But even old Isaac choked up at that, and I closed the door on him.

"How queer!" Lida said, looking at me. "So Isaac knew your mother? Have you lived always in Allegheny, Mrs. Pitman?"

"I was born in Pittsburgh," I evaded. "I went away for a long time, but I always longed for the hurry and activity of the old home town. So here I am again."

Fortunately, like all the young, her own affairs engrossed her. She was flushed with the prospect of meeting her lover, tremulous over what the evening might bring. The middle-aged woman who had come back to the hurry of the old town, and who, pushed back into an eddy of the flood district, could only watch the activity and the life from behind a "Rooms to Let" sign, did not concern her much. Nor should she have.

Mr. Howell came soon after. He asked for her, and going back to the dining room kissed her quietly. He had an air of resolve, a sort of grim determination, which was a relief from the half-frantic look he had worn before. He asked to have Mr. Holcombe brought down, and so there were the four of us sitting around the table: Mr. Holcombe with his notebook, I with my mending, and the boy with one of Lida's hands frankly under his on the red tablecloth.

"I want to tell all of you the whole story," young Howell began. "Tomorrow I shall go to the district attorney and confess, but I want you all to have it first. I can't sleep again until I get it off my chest. Mrs. Pitman has suffered through me, and Mr. Holcombe here has spent money and time—"

Lida did not speak, but she drew her chair closer, and put her other hand over his.

"I want to get it straight, if I can. Let me see. It was on Sunday, the fourth, that the river came up, wasn't it? Yes. Well, on the Thursday before that I met you, Mr. Holcombe, in a restaurant in Pittsburgh. Do you remember?"

Mr. Holcombe nodded.

"We were talking of crime, and I said no man should be hanged on purely circumstantial evidence. You affirmed that a well-linked chain of circumstantial evidence could properly hang a man. We had a long argument, in which I was worsted. There was a third man at the table, Bronson, the business manager of the Liberty Theater."

"Who sided with you," put in Mr. Holcombe, "and whose views I refused to entertain because, as publicity man for a theater, he dealt in fiction rather than in fact."

"Precisely. You may recall, Mr. Holcombe, that you offered to hang any man we would name, given a proper chain of circumstantial evidence against him?"

"Yes."

"After you left Bronson spoke to me. He said business at the theater was bad, and complained of the way the papers used, or would not use, his stuff. He said the Liberty Theater had not had a proper deal, and that he was tempted to go over and bang one of the company on the head, and so get a little free advertising.

"I said he ought to be able to fake a good story, but he maintained that a newspaper could smell a faked story a mile away; and that anyhow all the good stunts had been pulled off. I agreed with him. I remember saying that nothing but a railroad wreck or a murder hit the public very hard these days, and that I didn't feel like wrecking the Pennsylvania Limited.

"He leaned over the table and looked at me. 'Well, how about a murder, then?' he said. 'You get the story for your paper, and I get some advertising for the theater. We need it, that's sure.'

"I laughed it off, and we separated. But at two o'clock Bronson called me up again. I met him in his office at the theater, and he told me that Jennie Brice, who was out of the cast that week, had asked for a week's vacation. She had heard of a farm at a town called Horner, and she wanted to go there to rest.

"'Now the idea is this,' he said. 'She's living with her husband, and he has threatened her life more than once. It would be easy enough to frame up something to look as if he'd made away with her. We'd get a week of excitement, more advertising than we'd ordinarily get in a year; you get a corking news story, and find Jennie Brice at the end, getting the credit for that. Jennie gets a hundred dollars and a rest, and Ladley, her husband, gets, say, two hundred.'

"Mr. Bronson offered to put up the money, and I agreed. The flood came just then, and was considerable help. It made a good setting. I went to my city editor, and got an assignment to interview Ladley about this play of his. Then Bronson and I went together to see the Ladleys on Sunday morning, and as they needed money they agreed. But Ladley insisted on fifty dollars a week extra if he had to go to jail. We promised it, but we did not intend to let things go so far as that.

"In the Ladleys' room that Sunday morning, we worked it all out. The hardest thing was to get Jennie Brice's consent; but she agreed, finally. We arranged a list of clues to be left around, and Ladley was to go out in the night and to be heard coming back. I told him to quarrel with his wife that afternoon—although I don't believe they needed to be asked to do it—and I suggested also the shoe or slipper to be found floating around."

"Just a moment," said Mr. Holcombe, busy with his notebook. "Did you suggest the onyx clock?"

"No. No clock was mentioned. The clock has puzzled me right along. It didn't belong."

"Then what about the towel?"

"Yes. I said no murder was complete without blood, but he kicked on that—said he didn't mind the rest, but he'd be hanged if he was going to slash himself. But as it happened he cut his wrist while cutting the boat loose, so we had the towel after all."

"The pillow slip?" asked Mr. Holcombe. "Was it included?"

"Well, no. There was nothing said about a pillow slip. Didn't he say he burned it accidentally?"

"So he claimed." Mr. Holcombe made another entry in his book.

"Then I said every murder had a weapon. He was to have a pistol at first, but none of us owned one. Mrs. Ladley undertook to get a knife from Mrs. Pitman's kitchen and to leave it around, not in full view, but where it could be found."

"A broken knife?" Holcombe asked.

"No. Just a knife."

"He was to throw the knife into the water?"

"That wasn't arranged. I only gave him a general outline. He was to add any interesting details that might occur to him. The idea of course was to give the police plenty to work on, and just when they thought they had it all, and when the theater had had a lot of booming, and I had got a good story, to produce Jennie Brice, safe and well. We were not to appear in it at all. It would have worked perfectly, but we forgot to count on one thing. Jennie Brice hated her husband."

"Not really hated him!" Lida exclaimed.

"She did. She's letting him hang, isn't she? She could save him by coming forward now, and she won't do it. She's hiding so he will go to the gallows."

There was a pause at that. It seemed too incredible, too inhuman.

"Then, early that Monday morning, you smuggled Jennie Brice out of the city?"

"Yes. That was the only thing we bungled. We fixed the hour a little too late, and I was seen by Lida's uncle, walking across the bridge with a woman."

"Why did you meet her openly, and take her to the train?" Mr. Holcombe demanded irritably.

Howell bent forward and smiled across at the little man. "One of your own axioms, sir," he said. "Do the natural thing. Upset the customary order of events as little as possible. Jennie Brice went to the train, because that was where she wanted to go. But as Ladley was to protest that his wife had left town, and as the police would be searching for a solitary woman, I went with her. We went in a leisurely manner. I bought her a magazine and a morning paper, asked the porter to look after her, and in general acted the devoted husband seeing his wife off on a trip. I even"—he smiled—"I even promised to feed the canary."

Lida took her hands away. "Did you kiss her good-bye?" she demanded.

"Not even a chaste salute," he said. His spirits were rising. It was, as often happens, as if the mere confession removed the guilt. I have seen little boys who have broken a window show the same relief after telling about it.

"For a day or two Bronson and I sat back, enjoying the stir-up. Things turned out as we had expected. Business boomed at the theater. I got a good story, and some few kind words from my city editor. Then—the explosion came. I got a letter from Jennie Brice saying she was going away, and that it was no use trying to find her. I went to Horner, but I lost track of her completely. Even then we didn't believe things as bad as they turned out to be. We thought she was giving us a poor time, but that she would show up.

"Ladley was in a blue funk for a time. Bronson and I went to him. We told him how the thing had slipped up. We didn't want to go to the police and confess if we could help it. Finally, he agreed to stick it out until she was found, at a hundred dollars a week. It took all we could beg, borrow and steal. But now we have to come out with the story anyhow."

Mr. Holcombe sat up and closed his notebook with a snap. "I'm not so sure of that," he said impressively. "I wonder if you realize, young man, that having provided a perfect defense for this man Ladley, you provided him with every possible inducement to make away with his wife? Secure in your coming forward at the last minute and confessing the hoax to save him, was there anything he might not have dared with impunity?"

"But I tell you I took Jennie Brice out of town on Monday morning."

"Did you?" asked Mr. Holcombe sternly.

But at that, the schoolteacher, having come home and found old Isaac sound asleep in her cozy corner, set up such a screaming for the police that our meeting broke up. Nor would Mr. Holcombe explain any further.

CHAPTER 16

Mr. Holcombe was up very early the next morning. I heard him moving around at five o'clock, and at six he banged at my door and demanded to know at what time the neighborhood rose. He had been up for an hour and there were no signs of life. He was more cheerful after he had had a cup of coffee, however, and commented on Lida's beauty, saying that Howell was a lucky fellow.

"That's what worries me, Mr. Holcombe," I said. "I am helping the affair along and what if it turns out badly?"

He looked at me over his glasses. "It isn't likely to turn out badly," he said. "I have never married, Mrs. Pitman, and I have missed a great deal out of life."

"Perhaps you're better off: if you had married and lost your wife—" I was thinking of Mr. Pitman.

"Not at all," he said with emphasis. "It's better to have married and lost than never to have married at all. Every man needs a good woman, and it doesn't matter how old he is. The older he is, the more he needs her. I am nearly sixty."

I was rather startled, and I almost dropped the fried potatoes. But the next morning he had got out his notebook and was going over the items again. "Pillow slip," he said, "knife broken, onyx clock—wouldn't think so much of the clock if he hadn't been so damnably anxious to hide the key—the discrepancy in time as revealed by the trial, yes, it's all clear as a bell. Mrs. Pitman, does that Maguire woman next door sleep all day?"

"She's up now," I said, looking out the window.

He was in the hall in a moment, only to come to the door later, hat in hand. "Is she the only other woman on the street who keeps boarders?"

"She's the only woman who doesn't," I snapped. "She'll keep anything that doesn't belong to her, except boarders."

"Ah! That's the case, is it?"

He lighted his corncob pipe and stood puffing at it and watching me. He made me uneasy. I thought he was going to continue the subject of every man needing a wife, and I'm afraid I had already decided to take him if he offered, and to put the schoolteacher out and have a real parlor again, but to keep Mr. Reynolds, he being tidy and no bother.

But when he spoke he was back to the crime again. "Did you ever work a typewriter?" he asked.

What with the surprise I was a little sharp. "I don't play any instrument except an egg beater." I replied shortly, and went on clearing the table.

"I wonder—do you remember about the village idiot and the horse? But of course you do, Mrs. Pitman; you are a woman of imagination. Don't you think you could be Alice Murray for a few moments? Now think. You are a stenographer with theatrical ambitions. You meet an actor and you fall in love with him, and he with you."

"That's hard to imagine, that last."

"Not so hard," he said gently. "Now the actor is going to put you on the stage, perhaps in this new play, and someday he is going to marry you."

"Is that what he promised the girl?"

"According to some letters her mother found, yes. The actor is married, but he tells you he will divorce the wife; you are to wait for him, and in the meantime he wants you near him, away from the office where other men are apt to come in with letters to be typed, and pay attention to you. You are a pretty girl."

"It isn't necessary to overwork my imagination," I said, with a little bitterness. I had been a pretty girl, but what with work and worry—

"Now you are going to New York very soon, and in the meantime you have cut yourself off from all your people. You have no one but this man. What would you do? Where would you go?"

"How old was the girl?"

"Nineteen."

"I think," I said slowly, "that if I were nineteen and in love with a man, and hiding, I would stay as near him as possible. I'd be likely to get a window that could see his going out and coming in, a place so near that he could come often to see me."

"Bravo!" he exclaimed. "Of course, with your present wisdom and experience, you would do nothing so foolish. But this girl was in her teens. She was not very far away, for he probably saw her that Sunday afternoon, when he was out for two hours. And as the going was slow that day, and he had much to tell and explain, I figure she was not far off. Probably in this very neighborhood."

During the remainder of that morning I saw Mr. Holcombe at intervals, going from house to house along Union Street, making short excursions into side thoroughfares, coming back again and taking up his doorbell ringing with unflagging energy. I watched him off and on for two hours. At the end of that time he came back flushed and excited.

"I found the house," he said, wiping his glasses. "She was there, all right. Not so close as we had thought, but as close as she could get."

"And you can trace her?" I asked.

His face changed and saddened. "Poor child!" he said. "She is dead, Mrs. Pitman! She died in a New York hospital a day or two ago, giving premature birth to a child."

"Not the one at Sewickley!"

"No," he said patiently. "That was Jennie Brice."

"But Mr. Howell—"

"Mr. Howell is a young ass," he said with irritation. "He did not take Jennie Brice out of the city that morning. He took Alice Murray in Jennie Brice's clothing, and made up to look like her."

Well, that is five years ago. Five times since then the Allegheny River, from being a mild and inoffensive stream, carrying a few boats and a great deal of sewage, has become a raging destroyer and has filled our hearts with fear and our cellars with mud. Five times since then Molly Maguire has appropriated everything the flood carried from my premises to hers, and five times have I lifted my carpets and moved Mr. Holcombe, who occupies the parlor bedroom, to a second-floor room.

A few days ago, as I said at the beginning, we found poor Peter's body floating in the cellar, and as soon as the yard was dry enough I buried him there. He had grown fat and lazy, but I shall miss him.

Yesterday a riverman fell off a barge along the waterfront and was drowned. They dragged the river for his body, but they did not find him. But they found something, an onyx clock, with the tattered remnant of a muslin pillow slip wrapped around it. It only bore out the story as we had known it for five years.

The Murray girl had lived long enough to make a statement to the police, although Mr. Holcombe only learned this later. On the statement's being shown to Ladley in the jail, and his learning of the girl's death, he collapsed. He confessed before he was hanged, and his confession briefly was this:

He had met Alice Murray in connection with the typing of his play, and had fallen in love with her. He had disliked his wife intensely, and would have been glad to get rid of her in any way possible. He had not intended to kill her, however. He had planned to elope with the Murray girl, and awaiting an opportunity had persuaded her to leave home and to take a room near my house.

Here he had visited her daily, while his wife was at the theater.

They had planned to go to New York together on Monday, March the fifth. On Sunday, the fourth, however, Mr. Bronson and Mr. Howell had made their curious proposition. When he accepted, Philip Ladley maintained that he meant only to carry out the plan as suggested. But the temptation was too strong for him. That night, while his wife slept, he had strangled her.

I believe he was frantic with fear after he had done it. Then it occurred to him that if he made the body unrecognizable he would be safe enough. On that quiet Sunday night, when Mr. Reynolds reported all peaceful in the Ladley room, he had cut off the poor wretch's head and had tied it up in a pillow slip weighted with my onyx clock!

It is a curious fact about the case that the scar which his wife incurred to enable her to marry him was the means of his undoing. He insisted, and I believe he was telling the truth, that he did not know of the scar; that is, his wife had never told him of it, and had been able to conceal it. He thought she had probably used paraffin in some way.

In his final statement, written with great care and no little literary finish, he told the story in detail: of arranging the clues as Mr. Howell and Mr. Bronson had suggested, of going out in the boat with the body covered with a fur coat in the bottom of the skiff, of throwing it into the current above the Ninth Street bridge and of seeing the fur coat fall from the boat and be carried beyond his reach, of disposing of the head near the Seventh Street bridge, of going to a drugstore as per the Howell instructions, and of coming home at four o'clock, to find me at the head of the stairs.

Several points of confusion remained. One had been caused by Temple Hope's refusal to admit that the dress and hat which figured in the case were to be used by her the next week at the theater. Mr. Ladley insisted that this was the case, and that on that Sunday afternoon his wife had requested him to take them to Miss Hope; that they had quarreled as to whether they should be packed in a box or in the brown valise, and that he had visited Alice Murray instead. It was on the way there that the idea of finally getting rid of Jennie Brice came to him. And a method also, that of using the black and white striped dress of the dispute for the Murray girl to wear.

Another point of confusion had been the dismantling of his room that Monday night, sometime between the visit of Temple Hope and the return of Mr. Holcombe. This was to locate the scrap of paper containing the list of clues as suggested by young Howell, a list that might have brought about a premature discovery of the so-called hoax, and which had been mislaid.

To the girl he had told nothing of his plan. But he had told her she was to leave town on an early train the next morning. He gave her detailed instructions to wear his wife's clothes which he had taken with him, and to make herself up as nearly like Jennie Brice as she could. To carry out the deception, which he promised to explain later, she was to *be* Jennie Brice to young Howell. This he thought was safe, as Ellis Howell had only seen his wife once, and the girl was a fair actress herself.

His further instructions to her were simple: to go to the place at Horner where Jennie Brice had planned to go, but to use the name of "Bellows" there. And after she had been there for a day or two to go as quietly as possible to New York. He gave her the address of a boardinghouse where he could write her, and enough money to last until she could find work or he could join her.

He reasoned that as Alice Murray was to impersonate Jennie Brice, a Jennie Brice hiding from her husband, she would naturally change her name. And as the name Bellows has been hers by a previous marriage she might easily resume it. Thus, to establish his innocence, he had not only the evidence of Howell and Bronson that the whole thing was a gigantic hoax. He had also the evidence of Howell that he had started Jennie Brice to Horner that Monday morning, that she had reached Horner, had there assumed an incognito, as Mr. Pitman would say, and had later disappeared from there, maliciously concealing herself to work his undoing.

In all probability he would have gone free, the richer by a hundred dollars for each week of his imprisonment, but for two things. The flood which had brought opportunity to his door had brought Mr. Holcombe to feed Peter, the dog. And the same flood, which should have carried the headless body as far as Cairo, or even farther on down the Mississippi, had rejected it in an eddy below a clay bluff at Sewickley, with its pitiful covering washed from the scar.

Well, it is all over now. Mr. Ladley is dead, and poor Alice Murray, and even Peter lies in the yard. Mr. Reynolds made a small wooden cross over Peter's grave and carved "Till we meet again" on it. I suppose though that the next flood will find it in Molly Maguire's kitchen.

Ellis Howell and Lida are married. He inherited some money, I believe, and what with that and Lida's declaring she would either marry him in a church or elope, Alma had to consent. I went to the wedding and stood near the door, while Alma swept in, in gray velvet and a rose-colored hat. She has not improved with age, has Alma. But Lida, Lida under my mother's wedding veil, with her eyes like stars, seeing no one in the church in all that throng but the boy who waited at the end of the long church aisle—I wanted to run out and claim her, my own blood, my more than child.

I sat down and covered my face. And from the pew behind me someone leaned over and patted my shoulder.

"Miss Bess!" old Isaac said gently. "Don't take on, Miss Bess!"

He came the next day and brought me some lilies from the bride's bouquet, which she had sent me, and a bottle of champagne from the wedding supper. I had not tasted champagne for twenty years!

That is all of the story. On summer afternoons sometimes, when the house is hot, I go to the park and sit. I used to take Peter, but now he is dead. I like to see Lida's little boy. The nurse knows me by sight and lets me talk to the child. He can say my name quite plainly. But he does not call Alma "Grandmother." The nurse says she does not like it. He calls her "Nana."

Lida does not forget me. Especially at floodtimes she always comes to see if I am comfortable. The other day she brought me, with apologies, the velvet dress her mother had worn at her wedding. Alma had worn it but once, and now she was too stout for it. I took it. I am not proud, and I should like Molly Maguire to see it.

Mr. Holcombe asked me last night to marry him. He says he needs me, and that I need him.

I am a lonely woman, and getting old, and I'm tired of watching the gas meter. And besides, with Peter dead, I need a man in the house all the time. The flood district is none too orderly. Besides, when I have a wedding dress laid away and a bottle of good wine, it seems a pity not to use them.

At least I have kept my figure, and my mother's pearls are still in the bank. It seems queer, but Mr. Holcombe is quite well off. Besides, I have grown very fond of him.

I think I shall do it. It would be rather nice to ask Alma to the wedding, and see her face as I walk up the aisle.